The Secret Bridge

The Secret Bridge

HYWEL GRIFFITHS

Pont

For Steffan, Megan and Dylan

First published in 2013 by Pont Books, an imprint of
Gomer Press, Llandysul, Ceredigion, SA44 4JL

ISBN 978 184851 461 4

The Secret Bridge is Hywel Griffiths's adaptation
of his original Welsh novel, *Dirgelwch y Bont*.

A CIP record for this title is available from the British Library.

This book is published with the financial support of the
Welsh Books Council.

Printed and bound in Wales at
Gomer Press, Llandysul, Ceredigion, SA44 4JL

Prologue

January 1997

Parri pulled his cap down over his ears and rubbed his hands furiously. Despite the woollen cap, thick gloves, T-shirt, ordinary shirt, jumper, overalls, waterproof coat, two pairs of socks and wellies that made him look three times his actual size, he was freezing. The rain flowed from the hood of his coat, over his forehead and down his nose. Although the rain was hammering all around him, Parri couldn't hear it – all other noises were drowned by the rush of the river. He cursed to himself, muttering about being out on such a horrible night. He dried his face and looked at his watch. Ten o'clock. If he got a move on he could be sitting in front of the fire, a huge mug of strong, sweet tea in his hand, and watching *Match of the Day*.

He still had some jobs to do before that though. He needed to pop into the shed where the sheep were lambing, fill the water troughs and lock the gates. His father was already in the house, relaxing in front of the fire, his mother making him a cuppa. Parri quickened his steps through the mud and sludge towards the shed, opened the big metal door in one move and stepped inside. Although he could have found his way around the shed blindfold, he reached for the plastic light switch hanging down from the roof. Nothing happened for a few seconds, then the light winked, and winked again, and Parri caught a glimpse of one or two woolly heads looking to see what was going on. The light blinked quickly for a few seconds, before finally staying on and bathing the shed in white light. Parri pushed his hood back and, like a great shaggy dog, shook the rain from his greying hair. He looked around and realised at once that something was wrong. The small door in the furthest corner of the shed was swinging wide open.

Parri cursed once again as he realised that one of the sheep was missing, together with one of the lambs. A stall was open; the pallet that was once a wall lay on the floor, the water bucket on its side. The path beyond the door led out to the steep fields above the gorge and, although all the animals were familiar with the farm's winding paths, tonight those tracks were dangerous, especially for the little lamb. Parri couldn't afford to lose a single animal. He forgot all about the warmth of the fire and the tea and *Match of the Day* and forged out into the storm once again.

*

Although he was moving forward along the path, Parri couldn't really control his steps. He was pressing himself against the wind, one hand protecting his face from the rain, the other holding a small torch which only illuminated a few feet in front of him. He had long since given up trying to keep his hood in place. He looked down the slope to his right and saw the barbed-wire fence extending from one tree to the next. He knew that there was nothing beyond apart from the deep gorge through which the river was now rushing. He stamped his feet harder on the path and fought his way forward.

He thought he heard the sound of a lamb bleating and a sheep answering through the darkness in front. He pressed harder against the wind. He cursed again and took a deep breath. Thankfully, he came at last to an old wooden gate above the gorge, and leant against a gnarled oak tree next to it. He did not know what to do for the best. He saw the old rail track dimly through the rain. Although no train had travelled that way for years, the track was still there, the only straight line in this landscape of rounded hills and meandering rivers. Parri battled against the wind to walk towards the bridge which took the railway over the gorge. In the weak light of the torch he saw that some planks were rotten. Some were missing. The sheep and the lamb had managed to reach the other side by walking along a narrow strip of metal along the edge of the bridge. Parri sighed, before following them, holding tightly to the railings on the edge of the bridge and avoiding the brittle wood.

By the time he had reached the other side, sweat had begun to mix with the rain that drenched his forehead.

The sheep and the lamb stood still. Parri grabbed the lamb and turned around, trying to lead the sheep back across to the other side.

Suddenly, however, he was blinded by a bright flash. 'Lightning,' he thought to himself. 'Great.

That's all I need – walking across a rusting metal bridge in the middle of a lightning storm.'

He saw the light again, closer this time. What could it be? Stranger still, the sounds of galloping hooves filled his ears. Who could be out in this weather?

He crossed back towards the old oak tree that he had leant against earlier, feeling the sheep nudging the back of his leg as he pushed the little bleating lamb in front of him. He came to the oak and had to rub his eyes furiously. It seemed to be glowing red. Cautiously Parri extended his hand towards it. The wood felt warm, like smooth felt. He pressed a bit harder and his hand disappeared into the oak, right up to his elbow.

He looked back. The sheep and the lamb stood at the edge of the gorge; they looked scared. He paused for a second. Then, not knowing why he did so, he pushed his head, then his shoulders and his back and his legs through the soft oak and felt a warm shower pass over him. The sound of hooves was louder now and, as he stepped through the oak, he was blinded by the sun's rays. He shut his eyes tightly.

He opened them again, and regretted it immediately. A huge horse, black as night, was galloping straight for him, its nostrils flaring and its body wreathed in steam. Two people were bent over its neck, keeping low in the saddle. Parri opened his mouth to shout and, as he did, a number of things happened at once. An arrow whizzed past his right ear, and another through the pocket of his coat. He stumbled backwards and felt the warmth of the tree washing over him once again before his head appeared back on the other side, in the middle of the storm. His mouth filled with water, and he slipped to the floor.

Suddenly he heard something heavy fall by his side. A young man had jumped or fallen from the back of the horse. The young man had black shoulder-length hair, and a long pale scar stretching from his right ear to the corner of his mouth. His eyes were filled with fear and, in the second that Parri had to think, he realised why. Another person, a very pretty young woman, was still on the horse's back. The horse was now doing its very best to slow down. The surrounding trees began to bend, their branches flailing as the storm turned the rain into a thick, hard sheet and the white foaming water of the river was thrown up in all directions. Although the horse was trying to plant its hooves into the ground, it was sliding through the slippery mud towards the edge of the gorge. It struck the side of the bridge and its legs were hurled upwards. The girl on its back was thrown into the air and, as the poor animal fell towards the river, Parri threw out his arm to try and grab the girl's ankle. He caught her, and felt his muscles scream in protest. He held on and, as he felt his soaking hands start to slide, he saw another pair of hands grab the girl's legs and hoist her back up.

Feeling sick, Parri sank back against the oak tree that was now solid again. He looked over at the young couple, just far enough away from the edge of the gorge to be tearfully hugging each other.

Parri had no idea what had happened, no idea who they were, and no idea why an old oak tree had turned into . . . something else.

'I need a cuppa,' he sighed.

1

The History Lesson

'Jones!'

Owain Jones woke suddenly with the top of his pencil digging into his cheek. His teacher, Miss Hartley-Smythe, was standing in front of him, her narrow spectacles threatening to fall off her long nose. She was tapping her own pencil quickly on her arm, and she had a familiar, angry look on her face.

Owain swept his hair from his eyes. The rest of the class pretended to stifle laughter behind their hands and books.

'Well?' Miss Hartley-Smythe asked.

'Uuuum . . .'

More laughter.

'Which king of England had six wives?'

Owain realised that he had been sleeping. He had no idea for how long. The clock on the wall of the grey, miserable room told him it was ten past three. He remembered looking at it at three o'clock. He hoped that he hadn't been snoring.

Kieran, Mouse and Jase would be taking the mickey all night!

'Uuuum, Alexander the Great?'

'No, Jones, it was not Alexander the Great. You must have dreamt that.'

Owain heard more laughter all around him.

'It was Henry the Eighth. Now if you have joined us in the present, we'll move on. See me after the lesson, Jones.'

History lessons were so boring. He was completely confused with all the Henrys and Harrys, Elizabeths and Marys. The classroom, although grey and unwelcoming, was very, very warm, and the dark clouds of a summer storm were gathering outside. The teachers in the residential home where Owain lived never opened the windows. When he was in a better mood, he would joke to himself that this was to stop the boys from escaping. In truth, they were so worried about saving money that they kept the windows closed to save on heating bills.

Owain could not remember any home apart from this rather drab place on the outskirts of Liverpool: Flatlands Young Boys' Institute. Although he had no memory of life before the home, he did, sometimes, half-remember – or imagine that he remembered – green fields, the sound of rushing water and the smell of apples.

He knew very well that he had not been born in Liverpool. He spoke Welsh for a start, although he did not know how, or why. No one else in the home spoke Welsh, and the fact that he spoke English with a strong Welsh accent meant that he endured his fair share of leg-pulling; he did not really have any friends. Once a month, a little old woman named Mrs Ifans came to the home, asked him questions in Welsh, corrected his grammar and smiled at him kindly before leaving. That was another thing that he couldn't explain.

'Jones!'

Owain turned back from the window to face the front where Hartley-Smythe was tapping her pencil once again.

Despite the row he'd just received and the jeering from the other boys, Owain was smiling broadly as he walked back to his room. Because this was such a rarity it led to some very strange looks as he passed his fellow pupils. Owain didn't care – nothing could wipe the smile from his face tonight.

Tomorrow, Owain's class was taking a trip.

The oldest class went for a week-long trip every year, as some sort of gift from the home before they moved on to the local secondary school, perhaps to give the impression that the boys were being treated well.

The trip went to different places every year. Owain had heard exciting stories from older boys about canoeing, horse-riding and adventures in the middle of the night on the sides of mountains and in the depths of dark forests. Owain had not believed a word of it at the time, but now, on the night before the excursion, he found himself half hoping that something like that would happen to him. The best thing by far about the trip was that it was going to Wales. Although Owain knew he was Welsh, he had never been there. Not that he remembered, anyway. Tomorrow he would see Wales for the first time. He went back to his room and fell onto his bed as contented as he had ever been in his whole life.

2

Buses, Lorries and Tractors

Owain sat on the bus the next morning, his nose pressed against the window, half listening to the loud chatter around him.

'I hope they've got go-karts like last year!'

'And a PlayStation!'

'Yeah!'

'I'm having the first go!'

Owain shared their feelings, but he doubted that the others would let him do much with the PlayStation.

'Jones, you lookin' forward to going to Wales?' called a large dark-haired boy from the back of the bus.

'Yes, Mouse. You?' Owain was never sure whether Mouse was making fun of him.

'Lookin' forward to leaving you there, mate!'

Owain laughed along with the others. He had learnt long ago that was the best way to react. If he hit back, the jokes would get worse.

He settled into his seat. One of the springs had

broken and was digging into his back. He tried to move around to avoid it.

'Jones, stop squirming and sit still!' barked Hartley-Smythe from the front of the bus. Owain could see her bulbous eyes watching him in the rear-view mirror.

He sat back mutinously on the spring and looked around him. He played with the rusting ashtray on the seat in front – he just could not sit still.

With a cough, followed by a roar, the bus began its journey south. It pushed its way through thick traffic fumes, weaving through Merseyside's narrow streets. They were moving so slowly that Owain started to fear that the whole trip was a nasty trick, and that they would soon turn back towards the home. But slowly and surely the red-brick walls and narrow streets turned into leafy gardens and wide roads. A few trees and bushes began poking their heads above the concrete. The gardens became fields and the trees became hedgerows and small woods. Before long, the rickety bus was threatening to fall to pieces as it hit sixty miles an hour along the open road. As its speed increased, so did Owain's heartbeat. He looked around in wonder at the land rising steeply on both sides of the road, and the small streams twisting back and forth through the most beautiful green landscape that he had ever seen.

The pictures he'd seen in dusty geography books did not come close to capturing the life and excitement that he saw all around. Owain longed to jump off the bus and run across the fields and dive into the first deep pool he came to and start swimming.

His nose was pressed against the window once again. Something struck his back, and he heard Mouse laugh loudly behind him. The beady eyes at the front of the bus had seen nothing this time, of course.

After an hour or two, the bus began to slow down as the road narrowed and they were held up by some lorries and a tractor.

'Humph, farmers . . .' snorted Hartley-Smythe as another ageing tractor joined the main road in front of them. The farmer in the driving seat was nearly as old as the tractor itself, and a wild-looking black-and-white dog sat in the back, his red tongue moving from side to side. The bus driver sounded the horn to try and make the farmer pull in and let them pass.

'Beeeeep!'

The farmer took no notice; he didn't even show that he had heard. 'He must be deaf,' thought Owain.

The bus driver's patience was wearing thin. 'Beeeep-beeeep!'

Again, no sign. Owain heard him curse under his breath.

'Beeeep, beeeeeeeeep . . . beep beep!'

Still nothing. That was the final straw for the bus driver. To everyone's amazement, he steered the bus into the other lane, the gears grinding and the engine roaring. Very slowly, the bus began to overtake the tractor. Suddenly, Owain saw a massive lorry coming directly towards them around the next corner.

'Aaaargh!' At the back of the bus, Mouse had also seen it.

The bus driver stamped on the accelerator as he heard a faint beep-beep of protest from the lorry. Owain looked out of the window at the tractor, and at the man behind the wheel. He noticed at once a pair of unusually green eyes staring back at Owain in panic. In a second, the bus had passed the tractor and had pulled back into the correct lane and, as another angry beep-beep sounded, he knew that the lorry had also passed by safely.

Owain sat back in his seat, his heart pounding in his chest. The strange look on the farmer's face was still vividly in front of his eyes. But then, Owain thought, if a huge bus, and an even huger lorry, had just threatened to smash his little tractor into a million pieces and scatter them over the Welsh countryside, he'd look quite strange too.

3

The Crooked House

It was dark by the time the bus reached its destination, but Owain was still amazed by the difference between the countryside and the city. He was used to seeing bright lights winking at him on the horizon, and flames rising from the factory chimneys; sometimes he thought they looked quite pretty. The only lights that he could see here were one or two specks he guessed were isolated farms on the mountain sides.

'Wake up! We're here.' Hartley-Smythe's voice was rather trembly, and her face chalk-white. She must have been shaken by the grandstand seat she'd had to the incident with the tractor and the lorry earlier in the day.

Owain heard murmurs from the other boys as they woke up around him. He had not even tried to sleep. He wanted to remember every second of the trip.

As he got down from the bus into the car park, his breath caught in his throat. A biting wind hit him in the face. Apart from the sound of the boys chatting behind him, the place was quiet, and as still as the surface of a lake. Owain stood for a second and stared at the tall, solid-looking building in front of him. It had three floors, and a number of smaller buildings scattered around it. There didn't seem to be a straight line anywhere. The roof sagged towards the middle, and the end wall seemed to be leaning outwards, giving the place a rather unsteady look, despite the size of the rocks from which it was constructed.

'Shush now, boys.' Hartley-Smythe was like a mother hen clucking around her chicks. 'Jones, stop staring like a goldfish and get over here.'

Hartley-Smythe and the group of boys walked over towards the large wooden front door. Each of its oak beams was a different size, and stuck in the middle was an iron doorknob, three times the size of Owain's fist. The teacher grabbed it with her bony hand, and knocked.

After minutes of waiting, they heard bolts being pulled back, locks being turned, knots being undone, and, most worryingly, what sounded like a savage dog being restrained. The door creaked open slowly to reveal a huge man, who cast a shadow over Hartley-Smythe and half the group of dumbfounded boys standing in front of him.

'*Criw Glannau Mersi, ie?*' asked the man. '*Dech chi'n hwyr. Ma' criw Caerdydd 'di cyrraedd ers meitin. Rhys ydw i, gyda llaw.*'

Owain's heart leapt, and the giant must have noticed, because he bent his head slightly in his direction.

'P-pardon?' said Hartley-Smythe in an unusually small and timid voice.

'I said that you're late. The Cardiff lot have been here for a while. I'm Rhys. Come in. *Croeso*. Welcome.'

As Owain crossed the threshold, he saw Rhys's face clearly for the first time. He had a thick black beard, which was beginning to turn grey at the edges, large green eyes and a long nose. He frowned at everyone as they walked past him into the house – but Owain smiled at him as he stepped gingerly around him. He could have sworn that he received a small smile in return.

4

Bacon Butties

Owain was running as fast as he could through a huge church, his footsteps echoing loudly off the stone walls as he reached the door that led to the bell tower. He could hear the soldiers breaking down the door at the front of the building, and the sound of their heavy boots as they ran towards him.

'There he is, over by the tower!' one shouted, to the sound of swords being pulled from scabbards.

Owain stumbled through the doorway, slammed the door, locked it behind him, and began racing up the stairs in front. He had no idea where he was going or what he was going to do. He *did* know that he was afraid. He sped up the stairs, round and round and round and round until his head was spinning. He reached the highest floor of the tower and realised suddenly that he could go no further. His fright mounted as the soldiers hammered on the door behind him.

There was nowhere to run. Nowhere to hide either – no cupboard or chest to squeeze into as he had done before in Aber and Caernarfon. He panicked and grabbed the thick rope that hung from the large iron bell in the middle of the tower, and shook it. The bell began to peal loudly, making his ears ring, but still he could hear the soldiers' footsteps getting nearer . . .

Suddenly, somewhere close by, he could hear laughter. That wasn't right, thought Owain, as he slowly opened his eyes. He was lying in a bed, blankets up to his chin, the alarm clock on the bedside table ringing loudly. The other boys in the room were laughing at him.

'No idea what you were on about, Jones, but it sounded like a crackin' nightmare!'

'Uuuuugh . . .'

Owain sank back onto his pillow as the others, already dressed, left the room, still laughing.

After arriving the previous night, everyone had gone straight to bed. Mouse hadn't been at all happy with this, and Owain's belly was now complaining loudly. He washed quickly, got dressed, and walked out onto the landing. He was in a narrow, dark and winding corridor. He could hear the sound of voices and the chink of crockery coming from somewhere, and he rushed towards the steep stairs leading to the kitchen. As well as being very hungry, Owain knew he was late, and he could feel Hartley-Smythe's eyes looking for him through the thick walls.

Before he even reached the kitchen, the smell of bacon and sausages and toast rose to his nostrils and made him hungrier still. He entered a room where two long tables were set. On the left-hand side was a massive, solid-looking stove, with six noisy frying pans on top of it. Cupboards covered three of the walls and, on the fourth, two windows looked out on the back of the house. Chickens pecked here and there, six sheepdogs stretched lazily on the concrete floor of the yard and a few curious cows peeked over the nearest hedge.

Suddenly, Hartley-Smythe's voice rang through the room. 'Jones! Where have you been? Get some food and sit down there immediately!'

Owain went to collect a plate from the nearest cupboard. The boys from the home sat at one table; and at the other – looking at them rather dubiously – was a mix of girls and boys. Before

Hartley-Smythe had a chance to shout at him again for being slow, a short red-cheeked woman wearing an apron rose from the head of the table. She reached for Owain's plate and led him to the stove.

'This way, this way. Soon have you fed. Jones, are you? Welsh name, Jones. What's your first name then?'

'Owain.'

'Owain Jones? Weeell, you're a Welshman then, aren't you! Do you speak Welsh?'

Owain nodded.

'Nice to meet you, Owain.' The largest sausage he'd ever seen landed on his plate.

'I'm Anna, Rhys's wife.' Another sausage.

'Where are you from?' Two eggs.

'Who's your mam? Where's she from?' Four slices of bacon. Anna pushed the plate towards him with a broad smile, expecting an answer to each of her questions.

'Uuuum. Yes. I'm . . . not sure.' He smiled wanly. 'Sorry.'

'Don't be sorry, son! Sit down and eat! The Merseyside table is full, but there's room on the Cardiff table. They're Welsh like you are.'

Owain sat down opposite a boy with the

reddest hair he had ever seen. He looked as if his head was on fire. He looked at Owain and smiled and, although he had stuffed a whole sausage in his mouth, said: 'Allngghhhrrt bmrrrroy? Mm Nggeth.'

Owain looked at him, stunned. He felt a poke in his side.

'Hello. He's trying to say "All right, boy? I'm Geth." Geth the pig would be a better name for him, though. I'm Marian Gruffydd. Who are you?'

By now, Owain had also stuffed half a sausage, some bacon and an egg yolk into his mouth. He hadn't expected a question and tried to reply too quickly.

'Mmgnowaaaaingh. *Shw* – mnghm – *mai*?'

It was Marian's turn to look stunned.

Geth laughed heartily, reached over the table, grabbed Owain's hand and shook it enthusiastically. 'Great, butt! Good man! Nice to meet you. Haven't you eaten today or what? Ha ha! Hey, what are you doing with the Scousers?' He nodded towards Hartley-Smythe.

Gethin's laugh was huge; it echoed throughout the kitchen. From the corner of his eye, Owain could see Hartley-Smythe's thunderous face. He tried not to laugh, but failed.

'That's where I live. With the other boys over there.' Owain nodded towards the massive figure of Mouse, who was busy trying to fit two sausages into his mouth. He was sitting next to Kieran on one side and Jase on the other, his two partners in crime. Both were looking at Owain and Geth and whispering behind their hands.

'Good lads?'

'Once they've stuffed your head down the toilet once or twice, they're your friends for life!' Owain answered, half smiling, half frowning.

Geth laughed once again.

A tutting noise came from Hartley-Smythe's direction.

'Poor you, butt! Don't worry. Stick with us this week – we'll have some fun!'

Owain smiled at him.

*

Within half an hour all the children were standing in the farmyard. By daylight, Owain could clearly see the buildings and land all around them, the crooked side of the house, and the bedrooms that looked as if they were about to fall out of the upper storey. The eaves under the roof and the windows were also crooked. Smoke rose from two solid-looking chimneys.

The farm nestled in the shadow of a steep hill. Around them, the land rose sharply behind the farmyard and Owain could see drystone walls stretching towards the horizon. In the nearest field, a herd of cows grazed noisily, steam rising above their heads. On the higher slopes, white woolly spots were moving slowly to and fro.

Below the farm the slopes were gentler, the grass greener and the fields wider, with tall wheat and hay crops and a few orchards dotted here and there. Although he could not see it, Owain could hear the sound of a river flowing somewhere below. His eyes followed a line of trees that snaked left to right along the valley floor. He followed that line as far as he could towards the horizon until the landscape melted in a haze of mist and cloud.

A cockerel began to crow on the roof of a nearby chicken coop. The dogs in the shed closest to them were straining behind the gate, excited to see so many people. The Cardiff group stood on one side of the yard, and the Merseysiders, including Owain this time, on the other.

Now he noticed the adult with the Cardiff group. He wore a bright red coat and a green woolly hat with a bobble which waved back and forth in the wind. He wore a very old pair of walking boots; the laces were undone and dragged on the floor. He looked very untidy compared to Hartley-Smythe, in her brand-new hiking boots and expensive walking jacket.

Despite the frowns exchanged between their rival groups, Owain and Geth managed to smile at each other. Geth was pulling faces behind his teacher's back, making fun of his moustache, while Marian was poking him, trying to make him stop. Owain's smile widened as he watched them. The look on Hartley-Smythe's face, however, showed that she too had noticed their antics. She did not look amused. It was obvious that Geth's behaviour, coupled with the overwhelming smell of pigs and muck, was too much for her sensitive nose. Owain smiled even wider.

Rhys stood between the two groups. He wore a thick coat which looked as if decades of dust, mud and rain had changed its colour from green to some kind of blue-black. He had a pair of wellies on his feet and a thin length of plastic pipe in his hand.

'Right, *Croeso*.'

Owain sensed Hartley-Smythe tutting at his side. 'Welcome. *Heddiw mi fyddwn ni'n mynd am dro i fyny'r mynydd i chi gael dod yn gyfarwydd â thirlun Fferm yr Hafod.*' He turned to look at the Merseysiders. 'Today we will be going for a walk up the mountain so that you can get to know the landscape around the farm. *Dilynwch fi, peidiwch crwydro oddi ar y llwybrau a gwyliwch y cŵn – maen nhw braidd yn wyllt.* Follow me, don't wander from the path, and be careful with the dogs – they bite.'

He opened the gate and released the sheepdogs. They rushed out and began running around the children, barking playfully.

'Off we go!' With that, Rhys began walking very quickly – much quicker than Owain would have expected.

'Come on, children,' shouted the untidy teacher, 'race you to the top of the mountain!' He rushed forward without lacing his boots, half tripped over them and managed to save himself by grabbing a fence post seconds before falling face first into a large pile of cow dung. Owain and Geth looked at each other and grinned. They heard Hartley-Smythe say, 'Dear me. Come on, single file please. Let's go.'

Owain, Mouse and Jase followed Hartley-Smythe through the gap that led to the mountain slopes. The Cardiff pupils were already ahead, trying to keep up with their enthusiastic teacher, who was determined to stay close to Rhys and the dogs. The Merseysiders tried hard to keep up but Owain had already passed Mouse, who was breathing heavily and holding his side. Jase was still a little way ahead, but he too was beginning to struggle. Hartley-Smythe's long legs were able to keep pace with the leaders, but she was slow because she insisted on trying to avoid the cowpats and pools of water. Within minutes, Owain had caught up with the slowest of the Cardiff group, and he could see Geth's flaming hair and Marian's curls a few steps ahead.

'Hello,' he said, reaching Geth's side.

'Ows, man, how are you, butt? Fitter than your mates!'

'That's not too difficult, is it!'

Geth laughed. 'Where do you come from then, Ows? Before Liverpool, like?'

'Don't know. I don't remember where I lived before that, if I did live anywhere. The first memory I have is this home in Liverpool.' Owain tried to make his voice light.

'Oh, sorry, butt.' This was the first time he had seen anything other than a smile on Geth's face. 'What about your family then?' Geth's voice was so low that Owain had trouble hearing him.

'No idea. Every time I ask Hartley-Smythe . . .'

'Who?!'

'Hartley-Smythe – the one who's dancing in her posh shoes behind us. Every time I ask her she refuses to answer and tells me to stop being so ungrateful and cheeky.'

'Well that's not right at all, is it!' came Marian's voice from Geth's other side.

'What about you two?' Owain asked, trying to change the subject. He didn't like talking about his parents. It usually meant answering cruel questions from Mouse and his mates. Even when he was with Geth and Marian, he didn't enjoy being reminded that he didn't have parents, or a proper home. It was nice to just talk about nothing, he thought.

Marian began without taking a breath. 'Mum's a lawyer in Cardiff and Dad's a doctor. We live in Radyr. We've got a dog called

Bonzo, a goldfish called Jack, a rabbit called Flopsy . . .'

'And a budgie called Bob,' Geth added, rolling his eyes. 'I had her life history on the way up! Three hours in the bus.' He winked at Owain. 'She goes to Ysgol y Felin, and is going to Ysgol Pwll y Gaseg next year. Her favourite colour is red and her favourite member of *Hwyl* 21, whoever they are, is Siôn.'

Even Marian was trying to stop herself from laughing.

Owain laughed too. 'What about you, Geth?'

'Born: Cardiff Hospital. Raised: Cwm-nant-ddu-y-glo. Three older brothers. Dad cleans in the old colliery; Mam cleans everywhere else! Also going to Ysgol Pwll y Gaseg next year . . .' He pretended to be annoyed.

'Cool!' Owain loved hearing about other people. He started thinking about what would happen after this week ended. Would Hartley-Smythe let him write to Marian and Geth when they were back in the south, and he was back on Merseyside? Not likely.

Owain's train of thought was interrupted by Geth's voice. 'Hey! I know this Rhys bloke looks cool but how far do we have to walk? Bit boring, isn't it? If he told us some facts about the place, that would be something. What about having a look to see what we can find for ourselves?'

'No, Geth-in! Rhys told us to follow him and not to wander.'

'Yes I know, but, we're only on a hill farm in mid Wales, not a crocodile sanctuary! What do you think could happen? Look behind us; no one would notice if we slipped off. Everyone's too tired to notice anything!'

Geth was right. Even Hartley-Smythe had given up on checking where her feet landed, and there was no sign of Mouse or his gang. Ahead of them, a few of the Cardiff kids struggled after their teacher, who was striding about fifty feet in front.

'Mr Rhisiart. There's a legend for you,' said Geth.

'Hmmm.' said Marian. It was as if she was struggling between telling Geth off and at the same time agreeing with him.

'What about it then, boys? And girls, sorry, Maz.'

'Marian.'

'Yes, well, what about it? A walk on our own? We can catch up with the rest later on. Ows, you with me?'

'Uuuum.' Owain wasn't too keen on leaving the big group, but he wanted to stick with his two new friends.

'Don't, Owain, there's no need to break the rules.'

'Rules! They sounded more like suggestions to me!' Geth winked at Owain. 'Come on, Maz. Ows?'

'OK then,' said Owain, 'but what about going back towards the farm? We can find out what there is to see around the farmyard; at least then we'll have less of a row if we get caught.'

Geth and Marian looked at him. They were both surprised, but for different reasons, Marian because Owain was willing to break the rules, and Geth because the plan made so much sense.

'Excellent, Mr Jones. Back to the farm we go then. We'll have a look at the animals and tractors and all kinds of stuff. Coming, Maz?'

'Marian! Oh well, why not? I must say, this hasn't been quite as interesting as I'd hoped. I wanted to learn about the different types of grasses and reeds and trees and all about the history of the place.'

'Yeah, me too,' said Geth, rolling his eyes at Owain. 'Right, see those gorse bushes up there, on top of that little ridge? After we go past, jump behind them, and then crawl into the middle. Then we can wait until everyone else has gone and go back down the path towards the farm. OK?'

'OK.'

Owain's heart began to pound in his chest. He never enjoyed breaking rules, but he was having so much fun with his new friends.

'Jump . . . now!' Geth pulled Owain by his collar towards the bush. He was holding Marian's hand too.

'Ouch, Geth! You're hurting me!'

'Shush, Maz!'

5

Three Alone

Looking back at the path, Owain tried to ignore the prickly gorse on his back, arms and legs. Within seconds, he saw Hartley-Smythe and some of the boys go by. Her brand-new boots were very dirty and scuffed, and mud had sprayed up to her knees. She was out of puff but still managed to complain between breaths.

'Don't know . . . why . . . booked . . . crazy Welsh farmer . . . sheep . . . mud . . . refund.'

Owain stuffed his hand into his mouth to stop himself from laughing. He didn't see Mouse's huge legs passing by, or Jase's football socks. 'They must have gone past without me noticing,' he thought. He sensed Marian moving and heard Geth hiss, 'Stay!' He saw one more pair of legs struggling on up the hillside. Geth waited for two more minutes. 'OK, let's go,' he whispered.

With many an 'ouch' and 'oooh' as the gorse prickled through their clothes, the three struggled out of the bushes. 'OK, the coast is clear,' said Geth. 'We'll have some fun now, you'll see!'

They began to walk down the slope, side by side. The small ridge where the gorse bushes grew hid the three of them from any eyes that may have been looking back. After crossing the ridge, they sat down to relax for a second and enjoy the view. Owain was stunned to see how high they had climbed. They couldn't see the farm any more, just smoke rising from the chimneys and disappearing above the hill, and the line of trees along the river like a piece of cord on the valley floor. The heat of the sun had begun to burn off the morning mist and the green fields and valleys looked as if they stretched, like a smooth quilt, to the ends of the earth. On the near horizon the greenery darkened and the land rose, and Owain was sure that he could see, in the distance, the sun sparkling on snow.

'Wow!' he said, quietly.

'Wow is right, Mr Jones!' said Geth. 'Better than Cwm-nant-ddu-y-glo anyway! And Radyr, come to that. What do you say, Maz?'

'It's lovely. Come on, let's go down to the farm.'

Walking down was much easier and, before long, they had to stop themselves from running.

Rounding the large oak tree in the middle of the path, laughing at another of Geth's jokes, Owain stopped in his tracks. There, in the shadow of a rock, sat Mouse, Jase and Kieran, smoking.

'Behind the tree! Quick!' Owain grabbed Geth and Marian and pulled them behind the massive tree trunk.

Owain couldn't believe that the rest of the day was going to be spoilt by Mouse and his buddies. How on earth had they managed to slink away too?

'What shall we do, boys?' asked Geth, smiling. He didn't seem to mind at all. Marian, on the other hand, looked like she was sorry she'd left Radyr.

'What will those three do if they see us?' asked Geth again.

Owain thought for a moment. If he was alone, he knew very well what they would do – Jase and Kieran would hold Owain as Mouse gave him a wedgie. But he wasn't sure now, with Geth and Marian on his side. Geth's size (as well as his flaming hair) would be sure to make them think twice.

'They'd tell Hartley-Smythe straight away,'

answered Owain, 'and I'm sure that they would make a nuisance of themselves too.'

'What about finding another way back to the farm?' suggested Marian.

'Genius, Ms Gruffydd,' said Geth, mischievously. 'What do you say, Ows?'

'We don't have much choice, do we? But Rhys told us to stick to the paths, didn't he?'

'Yes I know, but the farm is only down there. So all we have to do is follow in that direction, and cross back to the right path once this lot are out of sight.'

Owain looked to his right, away from the path where the boys sat. He could see another track leading down the hill. Within a few metres it ran alongside a high stone wall which would hide them. 'OK, but we'll have to run if we want to get to that wall before they see us, won't we?'

'Yes. Leave that to me. Get ready.'

Geth grabbed a stone, looked at Owain and Marian to make sure that they were ready, and threw it back along the path that led up the mountain. Owain watched as Mouse, Jase and Kieran looked up sharply in the direction of the noise. He felt Geth nudge him in the back. He ran. The three of them reached the wall in a few seconds.

'Right, take two!'

The three friends strolled leisurely, safe under cover of the wall.

'What do you want to see on the farm then, boys? And girl, sorry, Maz.'

'Marian! I want to see the piglets, and the machines. I'm a bit hungry too, to be honest.'

'Me too!' said Geth enthusiastically. 'I could eat a horse.'

'You ate a whole pig for breakfast!'

'That was nothing, man. We've been walking for hours!'

Owain didn't say a word. The breakfast had been like a feast to him, and his stomach was still full.

The track now began to lead to the right, towards the wooded valley, and Owain could see a few more farms in the distance.

'I think it's best if we turn back for the farm now,' said Marian. 'I don't fancy going into those woods. Geth, you're the tallest. Look over the wall to see if there's another path.'

The wall was quite high, and Geth had to jump to see anything over the top. 'No, nothing.

There's too much bramble there. Thick too. We'll have to carry on until we get to the bottom of the hill and work our way back that way.'

'OK, come on then!'

6

Run!

By the time they reached the valley floor, the land was completely flat and lines of thick straight hedges stretched ahead of them.

'If we follow this hedge far enough, we'll come to a road, and then we can find our way back to Llanystywyll. I remember the way from there,' said Marian confidently, pointing.

'How on earth can you remember the way? It was nearly dark when we arrived!' said Geth.

'*I* wasn't snoring, like *some* people, Gethin!'

'No need to be like that. I was tired.'

'Don't you . . .'

'Hang on, both of you, no point arguing.'

'HEY!' A sudden shout came from the other end of the field. Owain could see a farmer at the gate, standing up on the wheels of his quad bike.

'HEY!' he shouted again.

'Run!' shouted Geth and, before Owain had a chance to think about what he was doing, he was by Geth's side, running as fast as he could towards the next hedge. He heard the angry revs of the motor bike and a dog barking madly. He kept on running. If they could reach the hedge, they might be OK.

Geth was a few steps in front of Owain and had already climbed the barbed wire and fallen into the brambles on the other side. Marian was next, and as she jumped onto the fence she slipped backwards. Owain grabbed her jumper and pushed her over the top so that Geth could grab her and pull her into the brambles. With the noise of the quad bike in his ears, Owain jumped over the fence, ripping his trousers before falling into the arms of the others. They turned to see the huge black-and-white face of the sheepdog, its teeth bared and its tongue moving eagerly from side to side. The dog was trying to squeeze its way through the fence and its wild barking had attracted the farmer's attention.

Before Owain could turn around, the farmer was already drawing near, his green eyes flashing under his cap.

'Quick!' Geth shouted. 'There's another gap up ahead. That mongrel will take a chunk out of our legs if we don't get a move on!'

Geth didn't look scared, but he wasn't laughing

either. More than ever Marian looked as if she regretted leaving Radyr. The three began to run again, as fast as their legs could carry them.

'Through the gate – come on!'

Geth led them to the corner of the field. There was no sign of the dog or its owner now. But, as they drew nearer to the gate, Owain's heart sank. It wasn't a road, or even a dirt track, but an old, dilapidated railway. The tracks themselves had rusted and snapped here and there, and briars had wrapped themselves tightly around the metal. Long grass grew on either side of the sorry-looking path.

'OK, what now?' asked Marian.

'We'll have to follow the track, won't we? It must lead somewhere. To Llanystywyll, maybe,' said Owain.

'Did you notice an old railway station when you were awake last night, Maz?'

'Ha, ha, Geth,' laughed Marian, slightly nettled, 'and don't call me Maz!'

'Off we go then, Ows,' said Geth with a wink. The wide smile was firmly back in place.

The three of them turned and began to walk. The track seemed to lead to the middle of the valley, towards the narrow line of trees hugging the riverbank. But, before they had moved more than a few steps, a determined bark sounded behind them. They turned, and saw the big black-and-white sheepdog leaping the hedge and speeding towards them. Without a word, they turned and fled.

Once again, Owain felt the wind in his ears and fear in his chest. Running along the track was very hard because they had to avoid the brambles and stray pieces of jagged, rusting metal. They saw the trees ahead of them, the railway tracks disappearing into shadow. They ran towards them and heard the sound of rushing water roaring in the canyon nearby. Owain couldn't imagine what might be waiting for them around the next corner, but felt that anything would be more welcome than the thing that was running full pelt behind them, so he ran on. He could hear the dog growling, and Marian struggling for breath beside him.

Suddenly they stopped in their tracks. They'd reached the woods and their eyes couldn't get used to the darkness fast enough after the bright sunshine. Slowly their eyes adjusted and they could see a bridge ahead of them, spanning a deep ravine.

'Come on! Don't stop!' yelled Geth.

'Where are we going?' shouted Marian.

The track that led over the old railway bridge had seen better days. Many of the wooden planks were rotten and the metal was rusted. Under the bridge, the water thundered through the gorge. If they stayed, the huge black-and-white dog would rip them to pieces. If they ran over the bridge, they could fall into the river and be dashed against the rocks. Owain didn't think much of the choice. This holiday had taken a frightening turn and he was sorry they'd left the rest of the group. For a very short second he missed Hartley-Smythe . . .

There was nothing for it but to run. The thought of the dog's razor-sharp teeth burying themselves in his leg was more than enough to send him on his way.

'Come with me!' said Owain. 'Keep to the side; step on the metal; the bridge will be stronger there. Don't worry, Marian: everything will be OK,' he added, noticing the fear on her face. He hoped that he was telling the truth.

He heard the sound of twigs snapping on the forest floor as the dog's paws swept over them. That was enough. Owain went first, putting his right foot on the metal and his left foot on the edge of one of the wooden planks. He moved as fast as he could, trying not to look down. He heard Marian behind him, shouting 'Oh no oh no oh no oh no oh no oh no' and Geth yelling 'Aaaaaargh!'.

A few planks were missing and Owain had to jump over the gaps. He reached the other side safely and turned back immediately to see where the other two were. Marian was hot on his heels. He grabbed her and pulled her towards him. Only Geth was left, with the dog following close behind. Teeth bared, it was leaping from plank to plank.

'Come on, Geth!' Owain shouted.

Geth looked up to see how close he was to the bank. As he put his foot on the last piece of wood and prepared to jump up, he heard a horrible splitting noise. A look of pure terror appeared on his face as he began to sink to one side. Owain jumped forward and seized his hand. Marian grabbed the back of Owain's jacket.

Owain's muscles burned, and his shoulders felt as if they were about to be pulled from their sockets. With his free hand, Geth grabbed a root under Owain's feet and struggled onto the bank.

Finally, the weight on Owain's shoulders lifted and he fell backwards on top of Marian.

'Phew, thanks,' croaked Geth.

But Owain said nothing. His eyes focused on the dog which had almost reached the end of the bridge. He was close enough to see the wild look in its eyes and the spittle around its teeth. The three friends tripped backwards and the cold sweat of fear broke out on their foreheads. With one final leap, the dog flew through the air towards them . . .

7

Strange Rain

Falling backwards, Owain could feel cold water flowing over his face. He felt a cold wind too, and there was a loud rushing in his ears. He could hear Geth shouting 'What the . . . ?' and the dog growling. He felt a hot breath on his face. The world turned black.

*

When Owain awoke later on, he had no idea where he was. His back was soaking and his legs ached. Something warm, wet and rough was moving to and fro over his face, and he raised his hand to stop it. It felt soft, like fur. He suddenly remembered the ferocious dog. His eyes snapped open and he scrambled to his feet, but his fear disappeared immediately. Although the dog was standing in front of him, it seemed to be smiling, and it was wagging its tail happily. It gave Owain's face another gentle lick from chin to forehead.

'Uuurgh!'

Owain heard a familiar chuckle by his side. Geth was sitting with his back to a large oak tree. He was laughing. Marian was next to him, smiling too, although she looked a little worried at the same time.

'Any chance of a hand, Geth?'

'By all means, butt. Come here, boy.' Geth whistled and clicked his fingers. The dog got up at once and rushed to his side. He lay down and let Geth stroke his belly.

'Thanks,' said Owain, very embarrassed to be on his back in a puddle of muddy water.

'My pleasure, Ows,' answered Geth. 'Least I could do after what you did. Didn't fancy a swim today for some reason.'

'What about me, Geth?' asked Marian. 'If I hadn't grabbed Owain's jacket you would have been a gonner!'

'Thank you too, Maz! Right, what's going on?'

'What do you mean?' asked Owain.

'You haven't noticed? It's dark. You haven't been out of it for a whole day, Ows! And, more importantly, the bridge has disappeared!'

'What!' Owain turned so fast that he almost fell over. Geth was right – the railway bridge had completely disappeared. There was no sign that a bridge had ever existed, and the level of the river was much lower too.

'What on earth?' Owain couldn't believe it. He pushed his hair out of his eyes, and turned back towards Geth and Marian. 'Where's it gone?'

'No idea, butt. Oh, and it's raining too. I know the weather in Wales is strange, but it doesn't change that quickly. I was worried about getting sunburnt earlier on.'

Neither of them looked as if they were pulling his leg. All kinds of scenarios flashed through Owain's mind. Could the bridge have been washed away? Was he still dreaming? Had he bashed his head on a rock and started seeing things?

Marian was talking again, in a determined voice. 'Boys, I don't want to be out in the middle of nowhere after dark. Could we get a move on back to the farm please?'

'But what about the bridge?' asked Owain.

'I don't know about the bridge. We'll see. All I really care about at the moment is getting back to the farm. It must be up this way somewhere.'

Owain looked at Geth. The look on his face said something like 'No point arguing with her!'

and he got to his feet. The dog jumped up too, tail wagging madly.

'Looks like this one's coming as well!' said Owain.

A steep slope faced them, but there was some kind of path leading up through the trees, perhaps made by a fox or a badger.

Owain's mind was racing. 'What's happening, Geth?' he asked, perplexed.

'I'm not sure, mate!' Although his friend was still smiling, he sounded uncertain. 'I never thought I'd say this, Ows, but Maz is right. We have to get back to the farm first. We might be able to work out what on earth has happened.'

'Yeah, OK. You're probably right,' said Owain.

The three of them started to climb the slope. But something else was worrying Owain about being on this side of the bridge, and he tried to work out what it was.

Marian must have seen the strange look on his face. 'Are you trying to figure out what's wrong?'

'Apart from the bridge, the weather, the time of day, you mean?'

'Yes. It's too quiet here.'

'What do you mean?' asked Geth. 'It was quiet on the other side of the bridge too.'

'No, it wasn't . . . not this quiet. Think. You could always hear cars on the road, planes flying overhead, dogs barking, sheep bleating. You can't hear a thing here.'

The more Owain listened, the more he agreed with Marian. But he didn't say so, in case he caused more argument. Their breathing and their footsteps sounded so much louder than usual.

They started climbing again.

At last they could see a way through the woods to some open ground. The land rose steeply in front of them and it was still drizzling. Without the shelter of the trees, the three children were soaked within a few minutes. They were still puzzling about the way things had changed so quickly. The weather *must* have turned while he was asleep, thought Owain. But that didn't explain the deathly quiet that was all around them.

All kinds of thoughts were going through Gethin's head too. First, he felt a bit guilty because it had been his idea to go for a walk. Second, he was determined to get Owain and

Maz back to the farm safely. Third, he was trying to work out what had happened. He wasn't too worried about the silence all around them. The important question was how the weather could have changed so quickly. Geth hadn't hit his head; he could remember everything. After Owain and Marian had grabbed him and pulled him to the riverbank he'd tripped forward, and suddenly he'd felt cold and there was rain falling heavily on his head. That wasn't a normal change in the weather. He turned the question over and over in his mind.

Marian was also worried, and was cursing Geth in her head. She wasn't concerned about the silence, or about the rain, but about reaching the farm in one piece. But, although she was worried, her mind was working overtime. She was now the leader. They had decided that they were not going to be able to get rid of the dog, so it had to become part of the team. They all felt that a large, ferocious-looking dog could be very useful! Marian had already decided that they needed to head north, uphill, to get back to the farm. She wore such a look of determination that neither of the boys had dared to argue, but followed her like two little lambs.

'Geth! Owain! I've found a wall!' she called after walking for a short while. 'It must lead back to the farm.'

'Woof!'

'You see, the dog agrees with me! Hey, we don't know his name yet!' Marian reached for his collar to see if he was wearing a tag. 'Yes, he's called Crach!'

'Bit of an odd name!' said Geth.

'Odd or not, that must be his name,' said Marian, noticing the way the dog pricked up his ears, wagged his tail, and gave a sharp, friendly bark every time they said it.

'Come on then, Crach, lead the way!' said Marian, sounding a lot happier now.

Owain and Geth stood still for a second and watched her slowly disappearing into the mist and drizzle. They raised their eyebrows, and walked quickly after her.

But even after walking for a quarter of an hour, they could still see no sign of the farm. 'I'm sure we'll be back at the farmyard before long, you'll see! This wall must end somewhere and there'll be a farm track that we can follow,' offered Marian, trying to keep their spirits up.

'There's something in front of us now,' said Owain. He had good eyesight, and could see a gap in the drystone wall and a track climbing up the hill.

'Great! I said so, didn't I? Everyone will be so glad to see us!' shouted Marian.

'Don't be too sure,' said Owain, sounding a little uncertain. He could hear Hartley-Smythe shouting at him already.

'Don't worry, Ows,' said Geth, sensing what was on his friend's mind. 'I'll tell them it was my idea.'

'You're right, Gethin,' Marian agreed. 'I don't know why we listened to you in the first place. This is all your fault.'

'I didn't force you to come.'

'What choice did I have?'

'Shush!'

Both of them turned towards Owain, annoyed that he'd dared to interrupt their argument. He raised his finger to his lips. 'What's that noise?' There was a tense expression on his face.

Neither Marian nor Geth said a word, but listened closely to see if they could hear what Owain could hear.

'Ows, I can't hear a thing . . .' began Geth. But

then he stopped suddenly and turned on his heel to face the farm track.

Badoom – badoom – badoom. Badoom – badoom – badoom. Badoom – badoom – badoom.

Now all three could hear the constant, rhythmic beats.

'Thunder and lightning?' suggested Geth.

'Or a landslide,' said Marian, fearfully. 'I heard on the news that there have been a lot of them this year.'

'I don't think it's a landslide.'

Badoom – badoom – badoom.

The noise got louder. It sounded like it was getting closer and closer. Owain turned around to face the way they had come, because a similar noise was coming closer to them from that direction too. Suddenly, he was afraid. He could see the same fear on the faces of Geth and Marian.

Badoom – badoom – badoom.

'Listen,' said Owain, speaking quickly now. 'I haven't got a clue what's happening, but I don't like it. We have to hide somewhere.'

All three rushed towards the stone wall. Crach was snuffling around their legs, as if he knew that something was wrong. He pricked up his ears and his tail was completely still. Geth started to climb the wall, grabbed the top and pulled himself over. Marian jumped up after him and, with one hard push from Owain, she fell to the other side. Owain heard an 'oomph' as she landed on top of Geth.

'Come on, Ows!' shouted Geth.

Badoom – badoom – badoom.

Owain grabbed Crach and threw him roughly over the wall. Then he grabbed the stones at the top and started pulling himself up. But as he stretched and threw his leg over, he saw a flash of black and white jumping over his head.

'Crach!'

In the tension and excitement Crach had jumped over Owain's head, back into the field.

Although Owain couldn't forgive the mean farmer who had chased them off his land, he didn't want anything to happen to his dog. He ran towards Crach as fast as he could and, slipping in the mud, grabbed him tightly and dragged the shivering animal to the shelter of a large rock. But Crach wasn't the only one that was shivering and shaking. The ground itself was vibrating.

BADOOM – BADOOM – BADOOM.

Owain dared to look up and saw a spike of Geth's red hair poking up over the stone wall. He waved his arms, trying to tell him to hide. He wasn't sure if his friend had understood or not, but he saw the red hair disappear.

BADOOM – BADOOM – BADOOM.

The noise was now deafening. Sheltering close to the base of the rock, Owain hugged Crach. Suddenly there were other noises mixed in with the loud drumming. From somewhere, horses neighed and men shouted as hooves hammered the ground, making it shake.

Owain looked up. Ten black horses, galloping fast as lightning. Each one was ridden by a helmeted soldier clad all in black and carrying a shield at shoulder height. The shadow of a sword hung from each man's belt, though some of the soldiers carried bows as well. From the other direction three smaller horses galloped towards them. Two were a mixture of brown and grey, but the middle horse was a pure, brilliant, beautiful white. Although these riders did not have shields or helmets, Owain could see that they too were carrying swords and bows. He suppressed the urge to shout a warning that they were about to crash into each other. It had not yet struck him as strange that he was watching two groups of soldiers on horseback, armed with swords, bows and arrows, in the middle of the Welsh countryside in the second decade of the twenty-first century.

As the first lot of soldiers realised that they were only facing a small group, a loud shout went up. 'Here's our chance! Don't let any of them escape!'

Owain heard the sound of metal swords being drawn from their scabbards.

A fearful cry came from the rider of the brown horse. 'Rhodri! Berwyn! Look out! Draw your swords!'

The horses slipped on the damp mud as the riders attempted to slow down. Suddenly arrows whistled through the air . . . men shouted . . . horses reared and snorted. Owain saw a horseman falling with an arrow in his throat. He turned away, revolted. Crach was underneath him, shaking with fear.

In a little while, Owain forced himself to watch the fighting once again. There were fewer soldiers now. Some of them were still on horseback but one of the smaller group was fighting toe-to-toe. The speed of it all stunned Owain: the swords and shields rose and fell so quickly, it was like watching a film on fast-forward. The sound of clashing arms echoed above the sound of wind, rain and horses.

Owain saw two soldiers on foot moving towards Crach, and another group moving back towards the gap in the wall. But it was the horseman fighting closest to Geth and Marian who was faring the worst. He swung his sword in his right hand but, obviously wounded, his left hand was hanging limply by his side. He had no control over the horse underneath him either and as it circled, mad with fear, the two soldiers attacking him had plenty of opportunity. His sword was struck from his hand. It fell to the floor and stuck in the mud. As a soldier plunged his sword into the rider's chest, his horse rose on its hind legs and fell on top of the stone wall, smashing it to pieces and crushing the rider. Owain realised that it had fallen exactly where Geth and Marian had been hiding. What if they too had been crushed? But Geth's red hair suddenly appeared a few metres away; he had moved just in time and had managed to drag Marian with him. Owain groaned with relief, but then saw that there was another problem – the soldiers had spotted his friends. He heard the shouts all too soon . . .

'Children! What on earth? Catch them, Malach.'

Another soldier leapt down from his horse and rushed at Geth and Marian.

'Run, Marian! Run!' shouted Geth before grabbing a stone and throwing it with all his might at the soldier. It hit him squarely in the face, and he stumbled backward.

'Ouch! I'll need some help here. Rhygyfarch!'

Rhygyfarch too leapt from his horse and grabbed Marian as Malach struggled with Geth. Within seconds, Rhygyfarch was on horseback again. Marian had either not fought, or perhaps she'd fainted, thought Owain.

'Let me go!' shouted Geth as he was dragged, arms and legs flailing, towards the horse. Malach struck him hard on the ear. Owain didn't think twice. He rushed from behind the rock. He didn't have a clue what he was going to do, but ran towards the sword stuck in the mud. He grasped the hilt, and tried to heave it from the ground. The sword was unbelievably heavy. But, with one massive effort, Owain succeeded in freeing it. He nearly fell over.

Rhygyfarch was now shouting at the other soldiers. 'Come on! Time to go!'

He spotted Owain preparing to swing the sword, and smiled through his dark beard. 'Oh, look. Someone thinks he's a soldier,' he mocked. 'Get him! Bring him with us! Maybe we can train him!'

As Owain mustered all his strength to swing the mighty weapon, he felt a strong pair of hands grab him from behind and lift him into the air. He let go of the sword and started to fight.

'AAARGH!'

As he fell to the floor, Owain heard a scream behind him. He looked up and saw Crach hanging off the soldier's leg, his teeth clamped to the flesh. The soldier shook his leg and threw Crach to the floor with a savage kick.

Owain heard a shout. 'Come on! Leave him!' From the floor, he could see horses galloping away into the mist. The soldiers had captured his friends and there was nothing he could do to stop them.

'Geth! Marian! No!'

Crach followed the horses for a little way, barking at the top of his voice, exactly as he had done when he was chasing the children over the farmland earlier in the day. But then he turned round and rushed back to Owain, sat next to him and licked his hand. Owain stroked him. 'Thanks, Crach,' he said, resting his head on the dog's back. He was shattered. Geth and Marian were on the way to who-knew-where, and his last meal, breakfast, felt like ages ago. Tears started at the corners of his eyes, and he dried them hastily. He rose to his feet with a great effort and a deep sigh.

Chaos was all around him. The bodies of the dead horse and its rider lay where they'd fallen and a number of other soldiers were lying lifeless in the mud. The water that flowed down the hillside was blood-red. Near the gap in the wall stood two of the smaller group of soldiers. One of them, a tall, strong-looking man, was leaning heavily on the wall; he looked as if he was struggling to breathe. The other sat on the floor. Suddenly, the figure rose, put a sword back in its scabbard and crossed towards the dead horse. Owain was stunned to see that the figure was a woman. She had fought as fiercely as any of the others. She sat next to the wall and began to cry, looking at the body of the soldier beneath it. Owain felt something moving under his arm and saw Crach trot over towards her, sit by her side and lick her hand. Although she looked surprised, she wasn't annoyed, and began to stroke him.

Owain wasn't as ready as Crach to trust the two soldiers. He picked up the sword and held it tightly.

The other soldier smiled at him sadly. His face was covered with scars, his greying hair, streaked with blood, was matted over his right eye. 'You won't need that sword, son,' he said.

As she heard the words, the woman looked up at him, and then at Owain, who could see that she was very pretty; black hair falling in long ringlets framed her face and her eyes shone through their tears.

'Who are you?' Owain was still doubtful about the two soldiers, but he slackened his hold on the sword. His mind raced as he remembered the strange things that had happened to him. He thought about the bridge that had disappeared the second they had crossed it, the changing weather, the ferocious battle with swords, bows and arrows and the two people now standing in front of him. They were staring at him, dressed as if they had just stepped out of a museum. On top of all this, Geth and Marian had been kidnapped by bandits. Anything could have happened to them . . .

'I'm Rhodri, and this is Gwenllian,' explained the man in a deep, kindly voice. 'Don't worry about who we are or what we do, for now. Are you hurt?'

'No, I don't think so,' Owain answered doubtfully. His grip on the sword slackened further. He was starting to get tired of holding it.

As if Rhodri had read his mind, he said, 'The sword's heavy, isn't it, son? Put it down for a second. I promise you that you have no reason to be afraid. If you come with us, we can look after you. We'll have to find something to eat. You can keep the sword,' he added. 'Berwyn won't need it any more.'

'What's your name?' asked Gwenllian.

'Owain.'

'Come here, Owain. You can have one of my spare cloaks to wear until we can find you something better. If you stand there like that much longer you'll catch a cold.'

Owain was so tired that he let the sword slip to the ground. He walked towards Gwenllian. She had pulled a dry cloak from the bag on her back. It had seen better days and many long journeys, but to Owain, who was soaked to the skin, it looked like the cosiest thing he had ever seen. Forgetting his reluctance, he sat by Gwenllian's side and let her wrap the cloak around his shoulders. As she put her arms around him to fasten the cloak, Owain relaxed against her shoulder. She rubbed his shoulders and his back to warm him, and he shut his eyes.

All the pain and sadness slipped from his mind and, for a second, Owain felt like he had a mother looking after him.

In an instant, he was sound asleep.

8

Sleep and a Plan

As Owain slept, wrapped in his cloak in the shadow of the white horse, Crach sitting near his head like some sort of untidy, hairy pillow, Rhodri and Gwenllian busied themselves around the battlefield. They talked in low voices, in order not to wake Owain, as Rhodri moved the soldiers' bodies and piled them together.

'What should we do with Berwyn, Rhodri?' Gwenllian asked sadly.

'We'll have to raise a cairn for him here. There's a place for him on the other side of the wall – we can use these loose stones here.'

'What should we do with those?' asked Gwenllian again, pointing to the dead soldiers.

'Burn them, I guess. Although God knows that's not what they would have done to us in the same situation. It's a shame to put Taran on the same fire as them.'

'I can't believe that Berwyn is dead, Rhodri.

We were the same age,' said Gwenllian, looking at the lifeless body in front of her.

'Neither can I, Gwen, but he understood the dangers. When you're my age, you'll have seen plenty of this.'

'I hope not.'

Rhodri continued to work. He collected Berwyn's bow and arrow which had fallen by his side. 'Owain can use these too. He'll need them before long, unfortunately.'

'Why do you think that?'

'You'll see. We'll have trouble trying to stop him saving his friends. You know who he is?'

'Yes, but . . .'

'You know then that courage and heroism, as well as wildness and impulsiveness, run in the family. God knows how he got here in the first place.'

'How much should we tell him?' asked Gwenllian quietly.

'Enough to stop him from running after his friends. But not everything, by any means. He's too young. He won't understand. It's not our place to tell him anyway.'

'But he has a right to know, Rhodri . . .'

'He does, but not now.'

'But . . .'

'No, Gwen, not now. Sometime, maybe, but not right now. It's unfortunate that he's landed here . . . for him . . . and for us. There was a plan to follow, and this isn't a part of it. We'll have to have a word with Parri when we take Crach back to him. Shame, too; he's obviously taken to Owain.' Rhodri's face split into a smile.

Gwenllian looked over towards Owain, who was still sleeping soundly. Crach looked up, saw them both staring at him and placed one paw on his new friend's forehead.

9

Galloping

The hills of mid Wales rushed by in the darkness. Owain opened his eyes and saw the shadows of leaves and patches of moonlight beneath him. The horses' hooves thundered as they galloped along the narrow, rocky road.

'Where are we?' Owain asked.

'On the Migneint,' answered Gwenllian, 'travelling towards Dolybrwyn Castle. Rhodri and Crach are in front of us.'

'Why? Where's Dolybrwyn?' Owain shivered. 'What about Geth and Marian?' he added quickly, suddenly awake. He realised that he had been sleeping behind Gwenllian. To make sure he did not fall, she had tied him to the back of the horse.

'You'll get all the answers in the court at the castle, Owain. Go back to sleep. We'll be travelling for another hour or two.'

'Court? What court?' thought Owain. Although questions still raced through his mind, he rested against Gwenllian's back, wrapped his cloak around his shoulders more tightly and fell asleep again.

When he woke for the second time the sun had risen. He felt its pale rays behind them, and saw the shadows cast by the horses and their riders on the road in front. The road ran along a narrow valley, high in the mountains. The grass was sparse in the fields on each side, and there were large boulders strewn everywhere, as if giants had been playing marbles. A small stream ran fast and white alongside the road, breaking over the large rocks that jutted here and there. At the end of the valley Owain saw the sun shining on a high tower. Underneath was a small castle, with white shapes moving to and fro near its base. Owain felt the wind pick up behind them and saw something red and yellow flying on top of the tower.

'There's Dolybrwyn,' Gwenllian explained. 'They're flying the flag of Owain Glyndŵr, Prince of Wales.'

Although so many strange things had happened to him over the last twenty-four hours, this sounded very odd to Owain. 'Is it Owain-Glyndŵr day or something?'

Gwenllian laughed. 'You could say that, Owain.'

Owain added this to the long list of questions he would ask when the time came. He was desperate for news of Geth and Marian – what had happened to them?

Riding straight-backed in front of Gwenllian was Rhodri, his sword gleaming in the sun.

As they drew closer, Owain could see the castle more clearly. It had been built on a ridge of rock in the shadow of the mountain, its walls as wide and grey as the mountains themselves. A huge gate was set in the wall facing them – the horses could walk through it easily even with the riders on their backs. The windows were narrow and most of them were boarded with wooden planks. A high stone wall topped by sharp stakes surrounded the castle. From inside, smoke was rising from a small cluster of wooden houses. Chickens and ducks pecked here and there, and others swam in a pool made by a stream. A couple of dogs lazed in a sunny corner, and the sounds of bleating sheep and snorting pigs came from somewhere nearby. Men walked to and fro, feeding the animals, tending fires and collecting vegetables. Some of them were sharpening swords, bending pieces of wood into bows and fitting metal tips to arrows.

'Don't move too much, Owain,' Gwenllian said. 'We don't want to excite them.'

'Excite who?'

'Them,' answered Gwenllian, pointing up at a ridge overlooking the road.

Owain's heart leapt into his mouth. Above them, men hid behind enormous boulders, their arrows fitted to bows pointing at the three riders. He couldn't understand how Gwenllian was so calm.

'Don't worry,' she said, noticing his worried tone, 'they won't shoot. They know Rhodri and they know me. But they've suffered a few attacks recently, and lost a number of people. They'll be friendlier when we get to the gate.'

Owain looked on as Rhodri reached the large gate in the stone wall and stopped to talk with a number of soldiers who leant forward to speak to him. He saw the soldiers nod and allow him to ride on. Once the horse was through the gate, Rhodri slipped from its back. Crach followed, and began to jump and circle around the soldiers. Owain and Gwenllian reached the gate, which was standing open. 'Rhodri must have explained who was behind him,' thought Owain. As they passed, he looked up at the soldiers' faces. Two of them had beards and deep scars, and their helmets were badly dented. They took no notice of Gwenllian, but they stared at Owain. He tried a smile, but did not receive one in return. He heard the gate shut noisily behind them.

'Come on,' said Gwenllian, who had jumped to the floor and was holding her arms out to help Owain. 'Quick, before too many people see you.'

Owain jumped down and Gwenllian led the horse in the direction Rhodri had taken. After sitting on the back of a horse for four hours, Owain was glad to walk for a while. He shook his legs and stretched his arms above his head.

'Did you get enough sleep?' asked Gwenllian with a smile.

'Hmmm,' Owain answered. 'Now will you tell me where we are and what we are doing here and . . . ?'

Gwenllian looked at him sympathetically. 'OK, I'll answer those two questions. The rest will have to wait, I'm afraid. This is the court of Dolybrwyn, in the mountains of Eryri. You know where Eryri is, don't you?'

'Of course, though Hartley-Smythe called it Snowdonia.'

'Well, Dolybrwyn is right in the middle, and

very difficult to find if you don't know the route. Do you remember the way we came?'

'No, I was asleep.'

'Yes, you were.' The two of them had now reached the stables. Rhodri had already tied up his white horse and had disappeared somewhere, and Crach had gone with him. 'Well, let me tell you, you'd struggle to remember the way even if you were wide awake in the middle of the day. That's why this place is so useful to Owain.'

'Another Owain! Owain who?'

'Owain Glyndŵr, of course! The chosen one!'

'Owain Glyndŵr?'

'Yes. You know his history, surely?'

Owain felt ashamed. 'I'm afraid I don't, I'm sorry. No one taught me anything about him. We learnt about Henry the Eighth and people like that in school; they didn't teach us anything about Wales, but I recognise the name, of course . . .'

There was a mixture of sympathy and shock on Gwenllian's face. 'No! Fancy not teaching Owain Glyndŵr's story. Don't you worry, boy. You'll know more than enough before long! Anyway, as I was saying, Dolybrwyn is useful to Owain at the moment because he's being hunted by most of the English army, and a few other armies are after him as well. They know that he has a court in Eryri, but as it's so well hidden and well protected, nobody has ever successfully attacked it. So that's where we are. Quite a long way from where we were last night, really. Which is a good thing, considering what happened.'

'What do you mean "*is* useful" and "armies *are* after him"? Where exactly are we? And what about Geth and Marian?'

'I think "What are we doing here?" was your second question.' Gwenllian's voice cut across Owain, as if he hadn't spoken. 'First, we're here to discuss our own matters. Rhodri and I were on the way back from dealing with an important problem when the soldiers attacked us. That's when you turned up. Second, we have to discuss what to do with you.'

'Me? What about me?' Owain sounded worried. 'And what about Geth and Mar–'

'Don't worry. Can you smell bacon? I'm famished. Come on.' Gwenllian grabbed him and turned him towards the castle door. 'One of the boys will look after Seren and Fflam.'

'Seren and Fflam?'

'The horses, of course. Wake up! You'll need to be on your toes today.'

10

The Prince's Court

Half an hour later, Owain was sitting at a large wooden table in an enormous hall. The sun shone outside, its rays giving light to the hall through its narrow windows. An open fire blazed at one end, burning logs as large as Owain himself, whilst red flames lapped at the chimney walls. He was sitting in front of a large bowl of *cawl*, next to a plate of thick bacon rashers. Despite his exhaustion, Owain had devoured several already and he was now dunking his bread into the steaming soup. The bowl was almost bigger than the sink in his room at the boys' home.

It was one of the best meals he'd ever had. He hadn't had a morsel to eat since his breakfast at the farmhouse. He also hadn't spoken for fifteen minutes.

Gwenllian was by his side, tucking in enthusiastically and looking at him now and again, smiling.

On his other side, Rhodri was eating as if he hadn't seen food for two weeks, and as if he didn't plan to eat for another two either. He sat back and drank a small measure of a golden liquid, sighing with tiredness and relief.

Facing them, on the other side of the table, was a rough but dignified-looking man. He had brown eyes and a white beard, and his white hair reached his shoulders. He wore a long black cloak, which was pulled tightly around his body. Brown trousers covered the long legs which he stretched out in front of him. He looked at the three of them in turn and smiled as he watched them eating.

At last, Owain finished his food and dared to steal a glance at the man opposite. He'd seen him once before, when they'd come in through the castle and were making their way along the dark, narrow corridors.

'Ah! Gwenllian! How are you?' the white-haired man had said, looking intently at Owain. He had led them to the kitchen, and then on to the great hall where they now sat.

Owain looked at him across the table. 'Thank you very much for the food,' he said, in a small voice. He could not explain it, but he felt nervous in the man's company. He had been very friendly, generous with his food, and had not questioned them in too much detail, but there was something about him that made the butterflies in Owain's stomach take flight. For some reason he found it difficult to look him in the eye.

'You're very welcome, son. You've travelled far to reach here. The welcome in Dolybrwyn is famous, although only a select few have proved it. You'll stay for the feast tonight, I hope?' He looked at Rhodri, raising his eyebrows.

'Thank you for the invitation. Of course we'll stay.' In a quieter voice, Rhodri went on, 'But we'll have to arrange for Owain here to get home as quickly as possible, or there'll be trouble.'

Owain cut in quickly. 'But we have to save Geth and Marian before that!' Then, as the old man looked in his direction, he began to explain more quietly. 'My friends, Gethin and Marian, have been kidnapped by the soldiers, and I haven't a clue where they are. I need to find them.'

Rhodri and Gwenllian looked quickly at Owain and then at the old man opposite. Owain saw the look. 'What?' he asked.

'There's a lot of things you don't understand,

Owain,' explained Rhodri. 'The situation is very complicated.'

'I know that it's complicated . . . I've got a long list of things that have happened in the last two days. Not one of them makes sense. But that's not important – the only thing that matters is getting Geth and Marian back safely.'

The man smiled at Owain again. 'Fair play to you, boy, for thinking of your friends, but we need to know a little more before we decide what to do. Go and get another bowl of *cawl* from the kitchen. We'll have the full story when you come back.'

'But what can we do?'

'We'll think of something. There are *some* perks to being Prince of Wales, you know.'

Owain stared at him, his mouth hanging open in surprise.

11

Ripping and Stitching

Owain returned from the kitchen carrying another bowl of *cawl*. He sat at the table and began to tell the story of the last few days, from the moment he left the home to the battle he had witnessed.

'You saw the soldiers last night, didn't you, boy?' said Rhodri.

'Yes.'

'Do you know who they were?'

'No idea. Are they important?'

'They're *very* important, Owain. They're called the Rippers. They are the reason that you are here at all. That old railway bridge is a tear in time. A rip in the fabric of the ages. It's a portal through which people can travel.

'I'm from the year 2090. I've got a family in that time,' Rhodri explained.

'I come from 2200,' added Gwenllian.

'I was born here,' Glyndŵr explained, with a cheeky wink in Owain's direction.

'But how . . . ?'

Rhodri went on. 'In the future – your future, that is, in the year 2070 – a group of people developed the technology that made it possible to travel through time by ripping through the material that keeps space and time together. They wanted to travel backwards and forwards through time in order to change things for their own purposes. All kinds of historical events have happened with the help of the Rippers. Horrible, wrong things. We travel back through time to undo the harm they cause, to close the tears in the fabric. That's why people call us the Stitchers. The battle is never-ending. Gwenllian and I, and Berwyn too, have been working in this century for over five years. We work with some special people in each age . . . people who understand.' He looked at Glyndŵr as he spoke.

'But how does the technology work?'

'Owain, there's no point in me trying to explain. Even if you were a scientist in your own time, you wouldn't understand. How would you explain to someone from the sixth century how a PlayStation works?'

Owain didn't speak for some minutes. He continued to look in shock at Rhodri, Gwenllian and Glyndŵr. 'I can't believe this,' he said quietly after a while.

'Think, Owain. How could the weather have changed so quickly? The answer's simple. It didn't really change at all, but whilst the sun was shining in your time, it was pouring with rain in this time. The bridge disappeared because it hasn't been built. It's quiet here because there aren't any cars, planes or televisions. People kill each other with swords because, unfortunately, that's what people do in this age. Believe me, Owain, when you crossed that bridge you went through a tear in time and travelled back to the fifteenth century. Today is 12 April 1401.'

A hundred questions flooded Owain's mind. Time travel? Wars across the ages? His head was spinning. 'But if you know about the tear over the railway bridge, why haven't you closed it?'

'Good question, boy. We've tried a few times, but failed. There's something strange about that rip, and a few others dotted around the country as well. Parri the farmer, the one who chased you, knows about it and has promised to make sure that no one gets near it. He'll obviously need a fiercer dog than this mutt in future!' said Rhodri, rubbing Crach's ears.

'OK . . . so . . . the soldiers on the black horses were the Rippers – the ones who kidnapped Geth and Marian? And you're the Stitchers?'

'Yes,' replied Gwenllian.

'And you battle each other across the ages?'

'You could say that but, to be honest, we're always one step behind, repairing the things that they damage, treating the wounds that they inflict.'

'But . . . how are there so many of them, and only three of you?'

'Three?' asked Glyndŵr sharply.

'We lost Berwyn last night.'

A look of pain came over Glyndŵr's face for the first time since Owain had met him.

Rhodri continued: 'There are more of them than us, anyway. They have the backing of the Government in 2070, and many others besides. We're a small band, always in retreat. There are around twenty of us through the ages. Gwenllian and I, and one other, are the only Stitchers in this century. Hywel and Esyllt are in the sixth century, Guto and Alaw in the sixteenth, and Iolo and Carys are undercover in nineteenth-century London . . .'

'There are some in the 1950s and 1980s too,' added Gwenllian.

'With so few people, all we can do is attack the Rippers when they least expect to have to fight. You saw last night what happens when we bump into each other. They win,' Rhodri finished with a bitter look on his face.

'You must have weapons and all kinds of technology that you can use? Why do you still use bows and arrows, swords and horses? Why not bombs, or lasers, or spaceships?'

'We can't, Owain,' said Gwenllian. 'Only a few people in each age know about us. Glyndŵr here, one or two of the poets and wizards . . .'

'Wizards?'

'Yes, and one or two others through the ages. Most people have no idea who we are. And that's how things have to stay. If everyone knew about us, the consequences would be disastrous. So we have no choice but to use swords and ride horses.'

Owain's mind was still spinning. 'OK, fine. But what can we do about Geth and Marian?'

Glyndŵr, Rhodri and Gwenllian looked at each other. 'Listen, Owain . . .' Gwenllian began. 'What you have to understand about the Rippers is that they are cruel. They have no conscience.

They'll do anything to get what they want. They'll do some things just for fun. Goodness knows what's happened to your friends,' she said, placing her hand on Owain's shoulder. 'I'm afraid you'll have to face the possibility that you won't see them again.'

'But . . . !'

'It's possible that they have been taken to Treffin Castle. Soldiers of the English army are there at the moment. They're fighting against our Prince . . .'

Glyndŵr inclined his head.

'. . . and the Rippers have been helping them for years. They must have been out spying or attacking someone last night. So, even if the Rippers haven't killed your friends, it's possible that the soldiers have.'

'No!' Owain shouted. 'Geth wouldn't let that happen. They're alive, I know it, and we have to try to help them!'

'But, Owain . . .'

'I can't go back to the twenty-first century without them! They're my friends! Everybody will be out looking for us. Well, they'll be looking for Geth and Marian anyway. What will I tell everyone?'

Glyndŵr was nodding. 'I'll send Ffinnant the spy out in the next hour or so to see what he can find. If your friends are still alive, we'll have to try to rescue them, won't we?'

Owain saw a flash of dangerous excitement in Glyndŵr's eyes, and the shadow of a smile on his lips.

'No! Think of the danger . . .'

'Rhodri, it's high time we showed them. We'll wait to see what Ffinnant has to say.'

'Thanks!' said Owain.

12

Poets and Spies

Glyndŵr walked across the patch of thin grass that separated the castle from the mountain. A small wooden hut stood there with two horses tied up outside. As he strode across the field, Glyndŵr passed soldiers and workers. All of them looked up and acknowledged him. The sun was high now, and the animals were either in the shade of the wooden huts or drinking water from the lake. On a large rock nearby sat a boy, not much older than Owain, busily sharpening a knife on a small flint.

'How are you, Ffinnant?'

'Sir?' The boy stood. He looked thinner than the reeds that grew near his feet, and his face had a keen, cunning look. He had weasel eyes, and cropped hair.

'Is Awel ready?'

'Yes. Twm shod her this morning. Do you need me to go out?'

'Yes, Ffinnant. I want you to go to Treffin

Castle. Contact the usual people. You need to ask about two children who are possibly being held captive in the castle. Are they dead or alive? If they're alive, where are they?'

'I understand, sir.'

'We need to know as soon as possible.'

'I'll leave at once.'

Ffinnant collected his things immediately. In a few minutes he was on Awel's back, clouds of dust rising as he galloped along the road away from Dolybrwyn.

The rest of the day flew by. Although Owain couldn't believe that he had travelled back in time, all the strange things that had happened to him now made sense. After Glyndŵr left the table, Owain had finished his *cawl* and sat there for a long time in Rhodri and Gwenllian's company, listening to them recount their adventures. He asked a thousand questions. Some got a reply, but others they flatly refused to answer, or changed the subject.

He found out a number of interesting things, though, including the location of other tears across Wales similar to the tear at the old railway bridge. According to Rhodri, there were places which led to specific years: a door in an

Aberystwyth hillside, a disused bus stop in Caernarfon, and a standing stone in Anglesey. Some funny things had happened, like an old woman walking through the bus stop into the middle of a medieval market. Rhodri had to go and save her before the locals tried to burn her as a witch.

The castle was bustling. Maids rushed to and fro – some ferrying buckets of water, others carrying pheasants, fish, and chickens into the kitchen. Some were carrying dishes from the pantry, and others bore large pieces of pork on their shoulders.

As Owain, Rhodri and Gwenllian walked through narrow corridors lit by flaming torches, the hustle and bustle shocked Owain. In the children's home, any noise was an excuse for a row, or worse. But here, it seemed as if everyone was trying their best to be as noisy as possible. The girls shouted at each other out of windows, or sang tunes while they worked. The sound of metal striking metal echoed from the smithy. Men called to each other and laughed as they sharpened their weapons, or worked in the garden or with the animals. In the orchard, children shouted as they ran around playing.

The sound of the animals was deafening – horses neighing, geese screeching, pigs snorting and cockerels crowing.

Owain explored the castle for a while, stunned at everything he saw. After a short time, he joined the other two and they went to sit outside and look down the valley. Rhodri wandered back and forth, feeding the horses and talking to some of the old soldiers, their scars hidden beneath their long hair and grey beards. They were going about their work quietly while the younger soldiers chatted and sang.

A number of people walked past them as they sat and talked. All of them nodded towards Rhodri and Gwenllian, as if they were used to having them around, but their eyes rested on Owain, obviously trying to work out who he was and what he was doing in Dolybrwyn. Nobody asked him outright, though; they must have accepted him as one of Glyndŵr's friends.

As the sun set, a cloud of dust rose on the long lane towards the castle. In no time, they could hear the sound of hooves.

'Here comes Ffinnant,' said Rhodri, as the horse slowed to a walk at the castle gate. 'He wasn't long.'

'*Shwmai*, Ffinnant?' he called loudly. The horse came closer. Then, in a quieter voice he asked, 'What news from Treffin?'

Owain looked up to listen more closely. His hands shook as he waited for news.

Ffinnant looked around, his weasel features moving quickly. 'Not here. Come to see Glyndŵr in a few minutes, and I'll tell you everything.'

By the time Owain, Rhodri and Gwenllian arrived at the castle hall, Glyndŵr and Ffinannt were already deep in conversation.

'Gethin and Marian are alive,' said Glyndŵr.

Owain sighed in relief. A load had been lifted from his shoulders. Tears came to his eyes, and he dried them quickly on his sleeve.

'But . . .' Glyndŵr went on, 'Finnant tells me that they are being held in the cells at Treffin Castle. I saw them once, when I was friendly with the people who used to live there. The cells were horrible. Cold, dark and wet. I can't imagine conditions have improved, not with the present occupiers. The castle is also impossible to attack. It's surrounded by steep hills, with a gorge on both sides.

'Gethin and Marian aren't the only ones being held there at the moment,' he added, looking at

Owain. 'There's another lad there. A boy called Mouse.'

'WHAT?'

'Why didn't you tell us about him before?' Glyndŵr's voice had hardened.

'How on earth . . .?' stammered Owain. 'I . . . I . . . I didn't know. He's from the same home as me. We're not friends. He hates me! He must have followed without us knowing!'

'He's not being held in a cell . . .'

'I bet he's told the soldiers all kinds of things to be friends with them.'

'Does he know that you're with us?' asked Rhodri.

'No idea. I didn't even know that he was here! What shall we do?'

'Nothing at the moment. The Rippers will expect us to try to rescue the other two of course,' said Rhodri.

'We have no choice but to attack,' said Glyndŵr, determinedly. 'We only needed an excuse.'

Owain opened his mouth to speak, but Glyndŵr had started talking again. 'We have to try. We can't let those three children rot. It'll be a chance for us to take Treffin Castle. I'll think of a plan tonight.' He turned to Owain, looking intently into the boy's eyes. 'We'll be sure to save your friends, and you'll be safe with us. In the meantime, enjoy the feast tonight.'

Glyndŵr continued his conversation with Ffinnant as Rhodri led Owain and Gwenllian out of the hall.

'We'll have to wait until tomorrow to hear the details,' he said, turning to Owain. 'Good news! Your friends are still alive!'

Owain smiled.

Rhodri went on. 'I suggest we do as Glyndŵr says, and enjoy the feast. We rarely get the chance.'

The tables in the hall had now been loaded with food, and all kinds of instruments had been placed at the far end. Rhodri, Gwenllian and Owain went to sit at one of the tables, where Crach was lying quietly.

A tall man with a rather unkempt look entered the hall carrying a jug. He noticed the three young people and came over to sit with them. 'How are you, Rhods? Gwen? And who are you, son?'

'Owain.'

'Owain who?'

'Owain Jones.'

Rhodri interrupted him. 'Owain, this is Iolo, the poet. Iolo, this is Owain.'

Iolo grabbed his hand and shook it so hard that an amber liquid spilt from the jug he was holding. 'Welcome, boy! Glad to see all three of you. Tonight will be a night and a half. I've got a few good poems, even if I do say so myself! Enjoy!'

He rose and moved to talk to two girls who were setting the table nearby. In seconds, the two were laughing merrily.

'Iolo's a character. An excellent poet, but a bit nuts,' said Gwenllian. 'He's right, though, tonight will be a good night.'

She wasn't wrong. Owain had never seen anything like it. The food was amazing – cheese and meat, fish and pasties, puddings, and drinks that warmed his insides.

Harpists played all night, and the strange, beautiful melodies wove their way through his head. Iolo rose many times and performed his poetry to the sound of the harp. Glyndŵr sat at another table, a wide smile on his face as he listened to the poetry.

After a while, the poems stopped, the music quickened and the dancing began.

At that point, Gwenllian decided it was time for bed. She led Owain up the castle stairs to a room in one of the smaller towers. The harp and the fiddle were still echoing in his head, and the poet's words were still conjuring terrible images.

When Gwenllian had found him some clean, warm clothes, and let him change, Owain slipped into bed and allowed her to lift the blanket over him. His eyes were nearly shut, and, compared to the lumpy pillows in the home, his pillow felt as light and comfortable as a cloud. He felt as if he hadn't slept for a month.

'Good night, Owain,' said Gwenllian, gently. 'Tomorrow will be here in a flash, so go to sleep immediately. And don't worry; I'll look after you.'

'Gwenllian?'

'Yes.'

'What will we do if the plan doesn't work?'

'Don't worry. There's no one like Glyndŵr once he gets an idea in his head. You can sleep tight.'

Owain and Gwenllian smiled at each other when, suddenly, they heard a snuffling and scratching at the base of the bedroom door. Gwenllian opened it and Crach rushed in, tail wagging, and settled at the foot of Owain's bed. They both laughed.

'*Nos da*, Owain.'

'*Nos da*.'

And with that, Owain closed his eyes and slept. Within seconds, he was snoring.

13

Poetry for Breakfast

Owain woke with the sunrise to find Crach licking his face. He coughed and shouted, 'Crach, get out of it, you silly dog!'

Owain got up, dressed quickly and went to the window. Smoke was rising from the chimneys of the huts. He rushed from the room and down the stairs to the kitchen.

'Here you are, Owain,' shouted one of the girls, handing him a bowl of porridge.

'*Diolch.*'

He took the bowl and continued into the hall where steam was rising from a large plate of bacon. In one corner of the hall, near the fire, Iolo the poet was sleeping with his head on the table. He was wearing exactly the same clothes as the night before and snoring louder than Crach; there was a half-full glass at his elbow. He and Owain were the only ones in the hall. Owain couldn't believe that Rhodri and

Gwenllian were still asleep. 'They must be outside, preparing,' he thought.

He sat quietly opposite Iolo, trying not to wake him, and started to eat his porridge. But, as his spoon hit the rim of the bowl, Iolo stirred. The snores stopped and the poet started to yawn. Suddenly, his head snapped up and he gazed around with a look of surprise. 'It's morning,' he said.

'Yes,' said Owain.

'What time?'

'About seven, I'd say.'

Another yawn. 'Uuurgh. It's too early. What are you doing up so early? I sleep until midday usually.'

'Well, I woke up, and then couldn't get back to sleep. I'm too nervous.'

'Nervous? About what?'

'We're going to Treffin Castle today to save my friends.'

'Bloody hell. How did they get there?'

'It's a long story, and I'm not sure I believe it myself.'

'Where are you from?'

'Um, Liverpool.' Owain wasn't sure what to

tell him. Did Iolo know about the Rippers and the Stitchers?

'Oh yes?' Iolo raised his eyebrows until they almost disappeared underneath his untidy hair. 'Will you go back there after you save your friends?'

'I'm not sure. Hopefully not.'

'Where else will you go in the twenty-first century?' Iolo asked, smiling.

'What?' Had he said too much last night? Who else knew?

'Don't worry, Owain; I know who you are, and I know Gwen and Rhodri well. I have a poem for Rhodri, actually. And yes, I know where you come from, or when you come from, rather. What kind of place is it, Owain?'

'Honestly, I prefer it here.'

Iolo smiled. 'But you don't belong here, do you, Owain? Everyone has to go backwards, or forwards, eventually. Go home.'

'I'm not sure if I want to go. I'd rather stay here, or stay with Gwen and Rhodri.'

'You'll want to go back once you've rescued your friends. And who knows, you may come back one day . . . you know how, I'm sure!' Iolo winked.

'Perhaps I won't go anywhere after tonight! I may be in a cell with Geth and Marian.'

'No you won't.'

'How do you know?'

'Because of the prophecy, of course!'

'The what?'

'The prophecy! The poets prophesied for centuries that Glyndŵr would succeed – before he was even born. He's the Son of Prophecy! And what's *your* name?'

'Owain.'

'Exactly. Owain. You're the second Owain, a second Son of Prophecy! You'll be sure to help Glyndŵr somehow! And if Glyndŵr succeeds, you'll have rescued your friends.'

Iolo had started enjoying himself. He drank from the glass at his elbow. 'Aaaah. I can see the flag flying over Treffin! We'll be singing about this victory for years. You'll get a fantastic poem from me, Owain.' Iolo started walking to and fro, seeing things in the hall that Owain couldn't see at all. He had such an ecstatic, wild look on his face, Owain couldn't help but share his excitement.

'Owain, I'm going to sharpen my sword. Tell

Glyndŵr to call me when the time comes. I'm coming with you today.'

Iolo rushed from the room straight into the kitchen, to the sound of shouts and screams and smashing crockery.

A few minutes later, Rhodri and Gwenllian entered the hall. 'What on earth did you say to Iolo, Owain?'

'Nothing, I just asked him a few questions! Why?'

'He's all excited. Talking about sharpening his sword. I don't think he knows where his sword is. Poets are supposed to talk, not fight!'

'Don't worry,' said Gwenllian, 'he'll have forgotten by the time we need to leave. Did you sleep, Owain?'

'Yes, thanks. Where have you been?'

'In the stables, making sure the horses are ready.'

'We won't be long now,' said Rhodri keenly.

Owain swallowed hard. His whole body was suddenly filled with a mixture of fear and excitement.

14

The Cave and the Tunnel

With Glyndŵr leading them on his black horse, the trip back to mid Wales was quiet enough. Glyndŵr rode in front of Rhodri whilst Gwenllian and Owain shared a horse behind them. Then came twenty of Glyndŵr's best soldiers, each one silent and unsmiling. At the back of the company rode Iolo, though he looked like he was still asleep.

Glyndŵr led the party over mountains, along winding tracks, through marshes and forests and along steep slopes until they came to the same river Owain had seen the day before.

Treffin Castle was in front of them, its shape clear and sharp in the moonlight. Owain could see the problem facing them. The towers were huge, with straight, smooth walls. The castle stood on a high ledge of rock jutting out into the valley. The river bent around it, flowing deep and fast through a rocky gorge, protecting the castle on both sides. The only bridge in sight crossed the river and led to a large wooden door protected by an iron gate. Only on one side of the castle was it possible to gain access without crossing the river, but Owain could see that a sharp precipice made this approach as dangerous as the others. He couldn't see a way in.

He began to feel like a fool. He had been adamant he wanted to come along, but he hadn't considered for a second what he would be asked to do. He had taken for granted that Glyndŵr had a plan. But, from the look on the others' faces, he doubted it. The group had come here to save his friends, and, against all common sense, they were going to try to do just that. What if Rhodri, Gwenllian and Owain Glyndŵr himself were kept captive in this horrible castle? It would be his fault. He felt an overwhelming urge to be back in bed, anywhere where he could hide underneath the covers. In Dolybrwyn, at Hafod Farm, even in Flatlands. Then he thought of Geth and Marian in a cold, dark cell in the depths of the castle. While Owain had been feasting, they had been suffering. He felt ashamed, and pulled his cloak tighter around his neck and grasped the staff he'd been carrying since Dolybrwyn. Rhodri must have noticed the strange look on his face because he asked with a smile, 'Are you going to take the castle on your own, Owain?'

'No! But we need to decide what to do. It looks so big and strong. How on earth are we going to break in?'

'There's no point trying to take the castle by force straight away,' said Glyndŵr. 'We would need ten times the number of soldiers to do that. We'll need someone on the inside to open the door and distract the soldiers. We can then attack through the front door.'

'Yes, but how will we do that?' Owain asked. 'The front door is the only way in that I can see.'

'Don't be too sure. There's another way, a secret way that the enemy doesn't know about.'

'Where?' Owain asked, excited.

'Do you see the rock under the castle?'

'Yes.'

'Well, there's a cave in the side of the valley above that rock.' Glyndŵr lowered his voice. 'With the help of our friends here,' – he smiled at Rhodri and Gwenllian – 'we'll find there's a covering over the cave that looks like stone. At the back of the cave there are steep narrow stairs spiralling down into the heart of the earth, connecting with a straight tunnel to the castle foundations. If someone can make their way in, raise hell, and open the gate for us, we can take the castle.'

'But how do you know that the tunnel is still there?'

'Don't you worry about that,' said Glyndŵr, with a sidelong glance at Rhodri. 'You'll see.'

'Why can't we all go through the tunnel?'

'Because it's so narrow, everyone in the castle will know we're there before we arrive,' explained Rhodri. 'It's a tunnel for a quiet attack by two or three, not a tunnel for an army.'

Owain thought of Geth and Marian once more, hungry and shivering in the corner of some cell. 'I want to go through the tunnel,' he announced defiantly. 'This is my mess, and I want to help clear it up.'

'No,' said Gwenllian firmly. 'You are not to go anywhere near the tunnel. You're a child, not a soldier. It's much too dangerous for you.'

'I'm not afraid!'

'That's not the point . . .' Gwenllian's voice was getting louder.

'Shh!' Rhodri hissed. 'Do you want the Rippers to hear?'

'It's not Owain's place to fight, Rhodri.'

'I'm not so sure.'

'What?' Gwenllian's voice was so loud this time that a flock of birds rose from a nearby tree.

'Ssshhh!'

'Sorry,' Gwenllian whispered, 'but what do you mean?'

'I think if Owain wants to help, we should let him.'

'Are you suggesting that we send him into Treffin Castle on his own then?'

'Of course not. We'll go with him, and distract the soldiers as he rescues his friends. I'm sure we won't be able to stop Crach following him either.'

Crach raised his head and made a small noise in the back of his throat. He didn't like all this arguing.

Gwenllian didn't look happy.

'Excellent!' said Glyndŵr quietly. 'Owain, you, Rhodri, and Gwenllian can go to the cave, and follow the tunnel to the castle. Once you're in, you can release the prisoners whilst Rhodri and Gwenllian,' – Glyndŵr looked at them with pride and a little anxiety – 'start raising hell. Owain, get to the door and open it. When we hear the noise, we'll attack. Listen, Owain,' he added, 'this is important. Once we're inside, and the battle has started, I want you and the other two children to get out of the castle. Don't wait for a second. Come back here. Once Treffin is ours, we'll come back here and take you to the rip in time so that you can go home.'

Owain didn't say a word.

'Do you understand?' Glyndŵr's voice was stern.

'Yes,' replied Owain.

'Excellent. Good luck. *Pob hwyl*! And thank you. The poets will be singing your praises tonight, you'll see. I'll tell the others.' He turned towards the group of soldiers, deathly quiet behind them, their dark clothes one with the forest, the moonlight shining on their shields.

Moments later, Owain, Rhodri and Gwenllian were creeping through the trees, Crach slinking at their feet. The moon lit the forest floor here and there and the shadows moved to and fro as the wind blew through the branches.

Slowly they climbed the steep cliff leading away from the castle. Owain had trouble controlling his breathing, and his heart was beating hard with excitement and fear. Two days ago he'd been struggling to stay awake, listening to Hartley-Smythe going on and on about the kings of England. Tonight, after travelling back in time, he was part of Owain Glyndŵr's army, creeping through the woods and getting ready to attack a castle. It was unbelievable.

He looked at Gwenllian. The wind was tickling her black hair, and her pretty features wore a defiant look. One hand was on her sword.

He looked at Rhodri, who had pulled his sword from its scabbard and was holding it in front of him. His eyes flashed in the darkness. 'Here we are,' he said finally, staring at a rock face in front of him. 'This is the cave.'

Owain looked at him and saw nothing but rock. Then he remembered what Glyndŵr had said about the Stitchers hiding the cave. 'How can we open it?' he asked.

'I haven't a clue,' said Rhodri.

'What?' Owain's voice rose a little.

'Ssshh!' hissed Rhodri and Gwenllian together.

Owain had imagined that there would be some complicated device protecting the cave. Something electrical, maybe, that this age hadn't yet discovered. 'Won't the Stitchers have used technology from the future,' he ventured, 'seeing as how they can travel in time to get it?'

'No, Owain. If we had done that, perhaps the Rippers would discover it as well. They can travel through time too, remember. We had to hide the cave to make sure the Rippers wouldn't find it. It's the same for a number of other locations up and down the country.'

'But how can you hide everything?'

'Poetry,' replied Rhodri with a smile.

'How on earth can poetry hide the cave?' Owain was starting to think they were pulling his leg.

'Well, not poetry exactly. It's a riddle in the form of poetry.'

'But why?'

'Although the Rippers can travel backwards and forwards through time, they show no interest whatsoever in poetry. We can use poetry to hide important things.'

'OK . . . but how . . . ?'

'Watch this.' Rhodri turned towards the rock and put his hands on it, moving them to and fro. 'Once upon a time, a Stitcher created this. We need to find the riddle that opens the cave, and solve it. We're lucky it's a moonlit night.'

Then Owain had a shock. As Rhodri's hands moved over the rock, words started to appear. In the moonlight he saw beautiful letters carved into the stone. Rhodri bent over and moved his hands over the base of the rock before standing back.

Four lines had appeared:

> To grow I first must fall,
> So large, but yet so small,
> I break and then by magic
> A dwarf becomes gigantic.

Owain looked in amazement at the words. 'What do we have to do?'

'Solve the riddle,' said Gwenllian. 'The lines describe something and we need to guess what it is.'

Owain studied the words, trying to make sense of them. 'What on earth grows after falling and is small and large at the same time? What grows after breaking?' He thought of all kinds of things, but none of them made sense.

He looked wildly at Rhodri and Gwenllian. They were both smiling again. 'Do you know the answer?'

'Of course. Don't you?' teased Rhodri.

'Don't worry, Owain,' said Gwenllian. 'We've had years of practice with things like this . . .'

Owain turned back to the rock immediately, determined to solve the puzzle. 'An egg falls in order to rise again and breaks before growing, doesn't it? Or a seed?'

'Try it!' said Gwenllian.

'What?'

'Put your hand on the rock and say the word.'

Owain walked towards the rock and stretched out his hand. As he touched the rock, he was shocked to feel heat coming from it. In spite of everything he had seen in the last few days, he still felt quite silly leaning on a rock face, saying 'egg'.

Nothing happened. Owain was disappointed.

He tried again: 'Seed!'

Once again, nothing. Owain thought hard for a moment or two, and an idea flashed into his head. 'Acorn!'

For a second nothing happened. Owain thought he was wrong again. But, suddenly, he saw the words disappear and he heard the sound of stone scraping against stone. A large section of the rock face moved to one side.

Owain turned back to Rhodri and Gwenllian and saw they were smiling widely.

'Well done, Owain!' said Gwenllian.

'Good lad,' added Rhodri.

Crach licked Owain's fingers to show that he was proud of him as well.

'Now the hard work starts.' Rhodri's voice sounded concerned. 'Listen, Owain. Before you enter this tunnel with us, you need to be sure that you really want to.'

'I'm sure. I want to help Geth and Marian – and stay to help you too.'

'We'll see about that,' replied Rhodri, glancing at Gwenllian. 'Listen,' he said again, weighing his words carefully, 'we don't know what we'll face in that castle. Who knows what the Rippers will do if they find us. The stories we've heard about the horrible things they've done! And there may be other things in there, besides the Rippers.'

'Like what?'

'I don't know, but I want you to be ready, that's all.'

'Don't worry,' said Owain with a grin. 'After all that's happened over the past few days, I think I can face anything. Shall we go?'

The three edged into the cave, Crach keeping close to their heels. There was enough room for Owain and Gwenllian to stand up comfortably but Rhodri had to crouch. For the first few yards, pale moonlight illuminated the cave. Rhodri began to explore, and found what looked like a pile of wooden sticks on the floor. As he raised them into the light, Owain saw that they weren't just pieces of wood, but torches.

Rhodri turned and pulled a small object from his belt. In seconds, the torches were burning brightly, casting ominous shadows on the wall.

Owain saw that the cave was quite a bit wider than he had previously thought. It had smooth, shiny walls. In the furthest corners, swords, bows and arrows were neatly stacked, alongside what Owain thought must be weapons from the future. There were piles of money too, and he walked over to have a closer look. He could see money dating from lots of different periods – large pound notes, coins that he recognised from the twenty-first century, gold and silver cards, some made from plastic and some from a material Owain did not recognise.

'This is a store for the Stitchers,' said Rhodri, grasping a dagger from the pile, along with a fistful of silver coins. 'If they arrive here in some sort of trouble and in a different time period, they'll be able to stock up on suitable weapons and money.'

Gwenllian was rooting around the back of the cave, torch in hand. 'Here are the stairs; come on!' she said excitedly.

Owain rushed over to her and saw that she had already begun to descend the steep steps. He followed her and, before long, could hear Rhodri's heavy footsteps following him. The steps were carved from the rock, each a different size and very slippery. If that wasn't enough, the stairs spiralled as they descended and, before long, Owain's head was spiralling with them. He heard Rhodri muttering behind him, but there was no sign of Gwenllian in front.

After what felt like hours, Owain reached the bottom. He tripped and fell to one side, grasping the wall in order to steady himself. Gwenllian was there, looking down the dark, narrow tunnel that lay before her. Rhodri joined Owain, with Crach, willing as ever, hard on his heels.

'Ssshhh!' said Gwenllian, as Rhodri's muttering echoed through the tunnel. 'Come on!' She led them towards the tunnel mouth. Once again,

Rhodri had to bend slightly. Like the stairs, the tunnel was also carved into the rock, its roof jagged and damp. There were signs that others had been here before them: torches protruding from brackets on the walls, an arrow or two, and a length of abandoned rope. Gwenllian's torch, and Rhodri's, were still casting strange shadows on the walls.

Suddenly, Gwenllian stopped dead in her tracks.

'What's wrong?' asked Rhodri.

'There's the end of the tunnel.'

'How do you know?'

'Look up.'

Owain saw a rope, and an old wooden ladder attached to the wall. It went right up to the roof.

'What are we waiting for? Up we go!' urged Rhodri. 'Once we get through the roof of this tunnel, who knows what we'll find! If we have to split up, don't wait for anyone. Follow the plan. Get the job done.'

'What about Crach?' asked Owain suddenly. 'He can't climb!'

'I'll carry Crach if I must,' said Rhodri.

Gwenllian jumped, grabbed the rope and started to climb. Rhodri lifted Owain so that he too could reach the rope. When Owain looked up, he saw that Gwenllian had already begun climbing the wooden ladder. He followed her. The wood was cold and damp, and some of the rungs bent under his weight but he carried on, though his arms were starting to ache. Gwenllian had now reached the roof and was looking back down at them. 'There must be some sort of platform there,' Owain thought as another rung bent under his weight. He reached the top and looked around. There was enough room for them to stand. He pulled himself over the edge of the platform and lay flat on the hard floor. Gwenllian was still looking over the side, waiting for Rhodri.

But instead of Rhodri, Crach's wide, hairy features appeared and he leapt over Gwenllian towards Owain.

Then Rhodri's face rose into view, and he was smiling.

At that moment came the horrible sound of splitting wood. Rhodri's smile instantly disappeared and he flung his arms over the side to try to save himself. Gwenllian grabbed one arm and started pulling. Owain grabbed the other, his body screaming in protest under the strain. They weren't managing to haul Rhodri up, but he wasn't sliding further down either.

Inch by painful inch, Gwenllian moved backwards, and eventually Rhodri was able to throw his leg over the edge of the platform. The three of them lay there, panting.

'That was close!' gasped Rhodri.

15

Fire and Whisky

Overhead, in the low roof of the cave, Owain could see a wooden door. He got to his feet and moved towards it. The others followed him and looked upwards.

'Right then,' said Rhodri, a little colour beginning to return to his face. 'I'll open this door slowly and have a look to see what's up there. If it's quiet, we may be able to risk it.' He reached up and opened the door a fraction of an inch. He peered through the tiny slit. 'It looks like some kind of store. Come on.'

Rhodri pushed the door open quietly and climbed through. He grabbed Owain's arms first and dragged him up. Crach then flew through the hole, thrown upwards by Gwenllian who was last to go through. The four of them crouched low and looked around. They were in a storage room of some kind, with barrels stacked on top of each other. Full sacks rested against the walls, and a film of dust lay over everything.

Rhodri crossed towards one of the barrels, opened it and smelt the contents. 'Whisky,' he said, quietly. 'Gwenllian, help me pour this.'

Owain looked at them in surprise. 'What now?' he wondered.

As quietly as possible, Rhodri and Gwenllian opened every barrel and poured the whisky over the floor. The golden liquid flowed to each nook and cranny, creating little channels in the dust. All four of them made for the storeroom door, taking care not to step in the liquid.

Rhodri reached into his pocket, pulled out a match, and struck it. 'We may as well start creating the diversion,' he said, flinging the match into the middle of the whisky.

The flames caught quickly and, before long, they'd started to spread.

'Come on, let's get out of here,' said Gwenllian, holding her sword in front of her.

They ran along a long, narrow corridor as fast as their legs could carry them. There was no one to be seen.

'Where . . . is . . . everyone?' asked Owain, breathing heavily.

'Feasting probably. I hope they won't notice the flames for a while,' said Gwenllian.

They reached a door. It was partly open and Gwenllian looked around it. 'Owain, there are stairs on the other side of this door, but there's a locked gate blocking the entrance. That's probably where the cells are. I can't hear anything on the other side, so when we go through, I'll smash the lock. You run down the stairs to look for your friends. We'll go on and cause more havoc. Once you find them, go straight for the main gate and open it.'

Owain swallowed. 'OK.'

Gwenllian put her arm around his shoulders. 'Don't worry. We'll see you outside. Ready?'

Owain nodded.

'OK, let's go.'

Gwenllian pushed the door wider open and charged at the gate beyond it, splitting the lock with one sweep of her sword. The gate swung open.

She stepped back. 'Go, Owain! Crach, stay! We'll need you.'

Owain ran through the door and down the stairs. Compared to the slippery, spiralling steps in the cave, these were wide and flat. His heart was beating so hard, he was sure that it was echoing off the walls. He was on his own again, and Geth and Marian were depending on him. The success of Glyndŵr's attack depended on him too. Owain couldn't hide the fact any more – he was afraid. He thought about what would happen if everyone was captured. Would he ever see the twenty-first century again? Would his Wales still be the same even if he managed to return?

He tried to concentrate on where he was going. The light from the room overhead had paled, and now the only light came from a few lonely torches. He was finding it difficult to see and he slowed down. Descending the last few steps, he was glad that he had. If he'd still been running, he would have run straight into a soldier sitting in a chair in front of him, snoring loudly. In his hand and around his feet lay empty bottles. He wore the uniform of a Ripper, similar to the soldiers Owain had seen two days before, but his helmet, sword and a bunch of keys lay at his feet.

'Hey!'

Owain spun around as he heard the familiar voice, and was greeted by Geth's shock of red hair. Behind the iron bars it looked like a burning torch. Geth still had a smile on his face, but he looked grey and tired. Marian was behind him, her hair unkempt and her face also grey, though her eyes sparkled when she saw Owain.

'Shhh!' Owain hissed as the drunken Ripper snored louder. He grabbed a torch from the wall and crept forward on tiptoes. He bent down and picked up the bunch of keys very carefully. He winced as the metal jangled. He crept towards the cell door.

'Hi, Ows! What on earth have you been doing? You look weird!' whispered Geth. Owain hadn't looked in a mirror for days, so it was very likely that Geth was telling the truth. 'How did you get here?'

'No time to explain, Geth. I'll tell you later. We've got to go. Are you well enough to try to escape with me?'

'Yes,' said Marian, weakly. She sounded as if she had had quite enough of this adventure.

'OK, which key opens the door?'

'The rustiest one.'

Owain held the key and put it into the lock. He tried to turn it, but couldn't. He would need some strength to open the door – that much was obvious. He tried again. The metal jangled louder still. Owain winced but the Ripper snored more loudly.

'Come on, Ows!'

He tried again with all his strength until, with a resounding clang that echoed from wall to wall, the key turned in the lock. Geth grabbed the door and shoved it open, before rushing through and pulling Marian after him. Suddenly he froze, a look of terror on his face. The Ripper was in front of him. All the noise had woken him from his drunken sleep. He opened his mouth wide and shouted: 'HEEEY!'

Before Owain could think about using his sword, Geth rushed past him, grabbed his torch and swung it towards the Ripper's head.

'Hmmph,' muttered the Ripper as he fell to the floor. To everyone's surprise, he was snoring again within a few seconds.

'Help me move this, Ows,' said Geth, moving towards the Ripper and grabbing his legs.

Owain went to help him. 'We'll lock him in the cell so that he can have a taste of his own medicine. He won't come after us either!'

They dragged the Ripper into the cell and slammed the door shut. Geth grabbed the key and locked it.

The three friends stared at each other and smiled a little nervously.

'You OK then?' asked Owain.

'I've been worse! What do you say, Maz?'

'Hmm, I'm not sure when I've been worse though. But yes, we're OK, thanks. These monsters haven't fed us much, but apart from that . . .'

'The main man – Rhygyfarch – came down to question us yesterday. Who we are, why we're here, blah blah blah. I told him straight – I don't have a clue! It was pitch black when we got here. Where are we, Ows?'

'It's called Treffin Castle . . . but there's too much to explain right now. We've got to get to the front of the castle and open the gate so that Glyndŵr and his soldiers can come in.'

Marian looked at him as if he had started losing his mind.

'I'll explain later!' said Owain. 'Be careful as you go. Rhodri and Gwenllian – new friends – are at the top of the stairs. They will probably have had to start fighting by now . . . and we've set fire to the cellar. It'll be dangerous up there.'

Marian stood still. 'I've just remembered – Mouse is upstairs! He followed us! He hasn't had an easy time, though. They've forced him to wait on them.'

'We heard,' said Owain, 'but I'm not sure what to do. We'll rescue him too, if we can!'

Geth grabbed the Ripper's sword and held it in front of him. Owain pulled his sword out as well.

'OK, Maz,' said Geth, 'stay with me.'

'I'll be OK – come on then!' The determined look was back and Marian's cheeks were looking a little rosier.

They began to climb the stairs – Owain leading, Geth behind him and Marian bringing up the rear. As they climbed, the light became stronger. Owain reached the top of the stairs and waited. He looked out. Thick smoke filled the corridor. He knew that there was no point going back the way he and Rhodri and Gwenllian had come, so he tried the other direction. The corridor rose slowly, with a number of small steps in front of them. They began to run, shouts, the clash of metal on metal and the barking of dogs filling their ears. Then, on the right, Owain saw a door standing wide open. Opposite was the main entrance of the castle. He ran towards it. As he did so he glanced towards the open door.

He paused. It should have been a wide and pleasant room with a high ceiling, long tables and a blazing fire. Instead, Rhodri and Gwenllian were standing in the midst of a large group of black-robed Rippers. Back to back, their swords flashing and spinning, his friends were fighting a number of Rippers at once. There was pain on Rhodri's face and Owain thought that he could see a tear in his tunic, near his shoulder. Gwenllian was also having a hard time dealing with all her attackers. At their feet, Crach was bouncing and spitting, baring his teeth and biting all the legs and arms that he could get his teeth around.

The Rippers swung their swords at him impatiently.

'Geth! We have to open the castle door! Rhodri and Gwenllian can't fight them all!' shouted Owain.

'Marian! Watch to make sure nobody comes out,' said Geth.

'OK!'

Owain and Geth stared at the door, trying to work out how on earth they could open it. There were so many locks and bolts, ropes and chains, it was very difficult to know where to begin. Geth pulled the keys from his pocket and threw them to Owain. 'You start on those locks!'

While Geth tried to cut the thick ropes with

the sword, Owain was having the same trouble he'd had with the lock on the cell door. Turning the key required a huge amount of effort. At last, one of the keys groaned in the lock.

Geth was still swinging the heavy sword, breathing noisily.

'Geth! Owain!' Marian shouted behind them, panic in her voice.

The two boys turned to see a woman in Ripper uniform coming towards them. She had short brown hair and the bluest eyes. She didn't look cruel, or even annoyed, just strangely fearful.

Geth and Owain jumped in front of Marian. 'Stay back!' shouted Geth, brandishing the sword.

The woman had shut the door behind her, leaving the battle behind. But, suddenly, the door opened again and a cruel-featured man stepped towards them.

'Aha, Non! You've found them! Good! Let us finish this once and for all.' He pulled a long sword from his belt and moved towards Geth, taunting him. He strode past Non and stood between her and the children, raised his sword and prepared to swing.

They waited for the impact.

Non rushed towards the man and grabbed him, pushing him into the castle wall. He struck it with a horrible noise and fell, unconscious.

The three children looked at Non, stunned. The fear had disappeared from her face as she looked at them. 'Owain?' she asked.

He nodded.

Non rushed towards him and threw her arms around his neck. Owain felt tears on his shoulder. He looked at Non's face, noticing the colour of her eyes. He began to shake. He couldn't believe it.

'Mam . . . ?'

'Yes, Owain.'

He had no idea what to say. Time seemed to stand still. Non smiled at him and hugged him close once again. Marian opened her mouth in surprise, and Geth's sword dropped to the floor with a clang.

Owain's feelings were rushing around his head. He had dreamt of this moment since before he could remember. On the one hand, he was very, very happy. There was no doubting the feeling of belonging, something he'd never, ever felt before. But all the events of the past few days were beginning to catch up with him, and the tears were threatening to spill . . .

'But how . . . ?'

'We don't have much time. I'm one of the Stitchers, but I have been spying on the Rippers for years. That's where I've been. It was me who spoke to Ffinnant yesterday, so I was expecting you. Where is Glyndŵr?'

'Waiting outside! We have to open the castle door!' said Owain, suddenly awake.

'OK!' Non grabbed the set of keys and started to undo the knotted ropes. Finally, she pulled the chain free and let it fall to the floor. She pushed the door open. Outside, the moonlight shone on the river and Owain could see the bridge clearly. When the light from the doorway spilled over the bridge, dark figures were visible, running full pelt, the blades of their swords gleaming brightly.

'But . . .' Owain paused as he realised that he did not know what to call his mother. 'Mam' was so unfamiliar. 'You're wearing Ripper uniform. Glyndŵr will attack . . .'

'No, he won't – Glyndŵr knows me well enough, Owain.'

At that moment, the first of the dark figures reached the door. In the light, Owain could see Glyndŵr's white hair blowing in the wind. At his side ran Iolo the poet, a big smile on his face. 'Well done, Owain!'

'Non! Where are Rhodri and Gwenllian?' asked Glyndŵr quickly.

'In the hall,' she replied, pointing towards the inner door. The prince smiled and rushed towards the door, giving it a massive heave and running headlong into battle, Iolo and his soldiers behind him. Owain heard shouts from the hall and the clash of swords.

Non grabbed the three children and ran over the bridge, putting as much distance as possible between them and the castle.

'But I want to help Glyndŵr!' shouted Geth.

'You've done more than enough already! Let the soldiers fight. We need to find a safe place to shelter,' said Non.

They ran as fast as their tired legs would carry them over the bridge towards a small building on the other side. It was some sort of shelter for the soldiers guarding the bridge but there wasn't much sign of them. Non led the children towards a few blankets and cloaks in the corner and forced them to lie down. 'You must rest. There'll be plenty of time to ask questions later. I'll find you some food. You two look famished.'

In no time at all, the events of the past few days, the shock and fear and excitement finally caught up with them. Geth and Marian slept soundly, but Owain continued to look at Non. She sat in a chair near the window, keeping watch.

She turned to him and smiled, the tears in her eyes plain to see.

For the first time in days, in years, Owain felt safe, and happy.

16

Crossing the Bridge

A large group of people walked down the steep slope towards the spot where the railway bridge should have been. Everyone was a little quieter now, even Glyndŵr, who had been talking enthusiastically with Geth about rugby for most of the journey.

Owain, Geth and Marian had slept in the small building at the side of the bridge until the morning sunshine had woken them. For a second, Owain thought that it had all been a dream. Then he saw his mother looking at him from the exact position that she had occupied the night before. She smiled at the three of them. She had found some food somewhere during the night and, as they enjoyed their breakfast of bread, cheese and apples, Non told them that Rhodri and Gwenllian were safe. Glyndŵr and his soldiers had defeated the army in the castle. Although a few Rippers had managed to escape, the castle was now securely in Welsh hands, despite the fierce fighting.

Then it was time for Owain, Geth and Marian to tell their stories. Non listened intently, obviously enjoying their company. In no time, a happy bark sounded from outside and a black-and-white bolt of lightning rushed towards them. Crach jumped into their midst and licked every available hand or foot. His tail wagged faster than ever as everyone petted him.

Then Glyndŵr, Rhodri and Gwenllian arrived. Gwenllian was holding a boy's hand.

Owain recognised him immediately. 'Mouse!' he shouted.

Mouse looked up, surprised to hear his name. 'Jones! Owain! Please, take me back with you!'

Owain smiled and nodded.

'Poor boy,' said Gwenllian, 'he's had a hard time with the Rippers. He was caught wandering the hillside above the railway bridge the morning after we met.'

Mouse was pale and his clothes were ripped. He looked from one face to the next, too scared to say anything.

Owain gave him a hug, and then they all started on their way, talking non-stop.

Rhodri, who was limping because of a nasty-looking wound on his leg, reported on the battle in the castle. Iolo was even starting to compose a poem to celebrate the victory.

Above all, it was a chance for Owain to talk to his mother.

'The first thing I want to do is say sorry. After you were born, we were attacked by the Rippers. Many Stitchers were killed, and your father took us to Dolybrwyn to hide. We decided that it wasn't possible to hide you because the Rippers would be sure to find you in the end. So we put you in the children's home in Liverpool. We changed our appearance and became spies. Your father is in the twentieth century – and has been for five years.' Although she was smiling at Owain, her eyes were teary.

'Can I come and live with you, Mam?' asked Owain.

A painful look crossed Non's face. She breathed deeply before answering. 'Not straight away, Owain. There'll be a lot of work to do for months yet, and it won't be safe for us for a while.'

Owain's face fell.

'But I promise you, I'll come to collect you when it's safe, and take you to see your father.'

Owain felt better. He could take another few months of life in the home if there was hope that his mother was coming to collect him.

The small group came to the exact spot where the bridge should have been, and fell silent.

The farmer with the green eyes was there waiting for them.

'Hello, Parri!' called Rhodri as Crach ran straight to him and licked his fingers.

'All right?' Parri nodded to Glyndŵr and smiled at Non.

'Can you make sure that this lot gets back to the farm?' asked Rhodri.

'You bet I can!' Parri looked fiercely at the children, then smiled.

'Have you seen Hartley-Smythe at all?' asked Owain in a small voice. He was very worried about what she would have to say about their unexpected adventure.

'Ha!' laughed Parri. 'She's been running around the place like a headless chicken, looking for you. You've been missing for days at our end, remember! Once they realised that you were missing, she went a bit nuts! She threatened to report Rhys to the police!'

Owain sighed and looked at Mouse, who

couldn't understand a word of what was being said.

But Parri wasn't finished. 'She came down here to look for you first of all, because the two others with this one,' – he pointed at Mouse – 'had told her that this was where they had seen you last. Apparently they were scared witless when they saw their friend disappear through the bridge, and they ran back to the farm as fast as they could to tell this Hartley-Smythe woman. Ha! I had a word in Rhys's ear and explained the situation. Since then he's been out pretending to look for you. I knew you'd be back before long,' he added, winking at Glyndŵr. 'The place is in uproar though; the police and rescue teams are out looking for you. But you needn't worry about Hartley-Smythe . . . she'll be as happy as everyone else to see you safe and sound!'

He turned to Geth and Marian. 'Your teacher has been worrying too, and your parents have arrived to help Rhys look for you.'

The three children looked at each other.

Mouse was cowering behind Owain and whimpering to himself that he wanted to go home.

Glyndŵr's voice drowned him out. 'Thanks for

everything, Owain. Come back to Dolybrwyn sometime, if you can find your way!' He shook Owain's hand.

'Thanks for your help,' Owain replied.

'The same applies to you,' said Glyndŵr, nodding at Geth, Marian and even Mouse.

'*Pob hwyl*, Owain, the best of luck. It was a pleasure to meet you,' said Gwenllian and kissed his cheek.

Owain blushed.

'Good luck, boy. We'll see you soon, you see if we don't!' Rhodri shook his hand.

'I don't know how to thank you.'

'Don't be silly.'

'Goodbye, Owain!' Iolo shouted from the back. 'The poem's nearly ready. You'll hear it next time.'

Non bent forward and whispered something in her son's ear. When she raised her head again there were tears in her eyes.

With one last look at the group, Owain turned towards the river and walked forward. He felt a warmth wash over him as he stepped into dappled sunlight. Suddenly, the bridge appeared in front of him. He grabbed its side and with his friends right behind him, he crossed over.

Owain, Geth, Marian and Mouse followed Parri's shadow along the same railway track along which Crach had chased them days before. They were all shattered, but pleased and excited to be on their way back to the present. There was a wide grin on Crach's face too as he ran and jumped between their legs.

'I can't believe that we have to go back to school,' Geth complained.

'I can't believe that we can't tell anyone where we've been!' said Marian.

'I can't believe that I have to go back to the home,' said Owain sadly.

'We'll save you! You saved us, didn't you? At least there won't be any soldiers with swords to stop us.'

'No, there'll be someone much worse – Hartley-Smythe! She doesn't need a sword!'

'Do you think we'll ever see each other again?' asked Geth.

'Of course we will. I'm going to make sure that I come down south soon. During the holidays, maybe.'

'But how, Owain?' asked Marian. 'Hartley-Smythe will never let you.'